CHRIS LYNCH
CYBERIA

SCHOLASTIC INC.
New York Toronto London Auckland Sydney
Mexico City New Delhi Hong Kong Buenos Aires

This book is dedicated to Christina
"Magnificent" Marchand. She's better than
everyone else, but she's very gracious about it.

This book was originally published in hardcover by
Scholastic Press in 2008.

ISBN-13: 978-0-545-02796-0
ISBN-10: 0-545-02796-9

12 11 10 9 8 7 6 5 4 3 2 1   9 10 11 12 13 14/0

Printed in the U.S.A. 40
First Scholastic paperback printing, January 2009

The text type was set in Adobe Caslon.
Book design by Christopher Stengel

I am sick of being watched.

And I'm sick of being listened upon. I'm sick of being monitored, traced, tracked, sensed, known about.

Parents are like that — I realize this. They want to know where you are and what you are doing every minute because they are concerned, because that's their job, because they love you. Where are you, where were you, where are you going?

My parents love me, I have no doubt, because I have it in writing. I have ten different types of electronic communication informing me that both of my parents do, in fact, love me, and how much. I have archived all of these.

So, I'm just home from school, standing outside my bedroom door, and I don't want to go in. Don't get me wrong — it's a fine, fine room. The best you can buy. It's just that I don't feel like being hounded. I want to slip in, flop out, and neither transmit nor receive any communication for a little while.

But that ain't gonna happen. It's not that my parents are in my room — it's worse.

I finally surrender after five minutes with my forehead pressed against the nameplate on my door. I'm sure I have ZANE embedded into my headskin now like a license plate, telling everybody my name backward whether I want them to know it or not. Though maybe if I become ENAZ, things will be different.

I turn the knob and step over the threshold, and it's like kicking a trip wire into some heavily guarded vault except the alarm is less of a siren thing and more of an arcade/disco/television newsroom.

Zane . . . Welcome, Zane . . . Welcome home . . . You have a message, Zane . . . How are you? . . . Why are you late? . . . You're awfully warm, are you unwell?

Can I tell you how much I hate that my room knows my temperature?

Very much, that's how much.

The whole place is buzzing and bleeping because my room is the buzzingest, bleepingest place you can imagine. I don't have decorations on my walls, no pictures, no wallpaper — I barely even have walls. I have screens. I have projections.

All of my electronic communication apparatus gets kicked on by my simply entering the room. I am wired by my anklet, into the drumming, humming heart of my family's central control system. My little black band, strapped to my leg and connected with a wire that goes right under my skin and on into who knows what depths of me, runs my whole life. Without even asking me.

So when I step into the room, the computer comes on, the radioweb comes on, the televisual walls come on, split into a multitude of screens that can beam the world's hot spots right to me. Sometimes I get close-ups of my driveway. Sometimes I get the real-time view of my school gates. Sometimes I get all the action of my cat hunting out in the garden. I get music and sports scoreboards — even though I don't like sports — and Spanish lessons synchronized to what I am working on in school.

The first panel on the wall, just as I walk in, is my personal barometer. Just numbers and letters blinking on a screen, keeping a running tab on my physical status. In addition to my temperature — which happens now to be 98.7, so really, why the nagging, Room? — it shows my heart rate and blood pressure and glucose levels. The barometer also monitors all variety of vitamins, minerals, chemicals, and microscopic bio-organisms that mean nothing to me, but apparently it's all important for keeping me alive. My calcium and vitamin A are down at the moment, which means my dinner menu is already being polluted with cauliflower and stinky cheese sauce. Then there's my personal favorite stat, which I like to call the JohnMon. Please, have a peek:

Anticipated next necessary lavatory visit: seven minutes.
Yup.

Isn't that nice of Wall? Thank you, Wall. Just watch. Come seven minutes, I'm holding it, just for spite.

They talk to each other, my anklet and the central control system, not to me. They talk *about* me, *around* me. And the results explode all over my walls.

It's no wonder I get fuzzy sometimes, on where it all ends and I begin.

The screens also provide me with the family unit. My mother is on the televisual wall. Not just here, but on other people's televisuals, too. She's a Newsmama. My father is That Voice on the national radioweb, explaining the modern world to itself with a massive authority that makes everyone believe him. And he is so popular his radioweb program is on the televisual at the same time. It doesn't make for gripping televisuals, watching him talk into a mic, but his ratings are great because, I guess, people just need to be reassured that he actually exists behind That Voice.

So I get to watch my parents work on screens two and four. And then, on screen five, I get a personal greeting from my mother, running right alongside professional Mom, asking me about my day and telling me to burn some ticks out of my dog, Hugo. Screen six has my stupid face, because wherever I go in here, it follows me. Presumably this is my folks' makeup call for not providing any actual siblings for me to play with, but really I can't help noticing there is a difference.

Their other response was animals. In the early days,

every birthday, holiday, rainy day, slow news day, I'd get a new pet to keep me company, bring me out of my shell, and emotionally subdue me so I didn't become too much of a pain. At some point, they must have decided that plan wasn't working since I guess I remained shell-bound and emotionally shapeless. They switched tack, stopped with the pets — though, funny enough, they all still hang around — and went techno on me. They were taking no chances — if I didn't connect sufficiently with the beasts, I'd be connected by a good old wiring-up. Hello, Room.

It's very lively and conversational, my room. A voice comes out of nowhere — well, not nowhere, exactly, but the giant speaker that is my ceiling — to gently tell me things I need to know. I can even program it to speak in the voice of my choice: my dad's, my mom's, even my own. Right now I have it set to scramble, which is random bits of the thousands of voices it knows, chipped together in no particular order. It's kind of freaky, but it doesn't get monotonous.

You have a communiqué, Speaker says. Speaker can be very snotty.

"You mean I have a message, Speaker? A message, is that what you mean? *Communiqué* sounds like a dessert. It's not time for dessert. Do you mean a message, or is dinner served backward tonight?"

Speaker does not like repeating itself.

I go to my desk, to my actual old-fashioned computer. The thing is almost as big as my bathtub, and just about as versatile. It is madly out-of-date, but it does what I need when all I need is to read or write. My parents fight hard to have the old embarrassment dragged away during our every-six-month technology overhaul, but this is the one place where I hold my ground. I have had it since I was old enough to foul the keys with my peanut butter fingers, and it has sentimental value for me. The background on the screen is an undoctored photo of Hugo's amazing face, which looks as if I drew him by making dots and lines in the snow. I've had Hugo and the computer for exactly the same amount of time, and my parents don't get my attachment to either.

They don't understand, because I don't really tell them. I don't tell them because they wouldn't understand. This old box computer is the constant, the thing that when I wake up (and when I wake up, the whole *room* wakes up), it connects me. To me six months ago, and six months before that. It's the only piece of gear in the place, actually, that I feel some control over. I feel I am the one working it, instead of it working me.

Hi, Zany.

I slump over at the words on the screen.

Then Speaker nags at me from above. *Back straight. Shoulders square, spine straight at the keyboard at all times.*

I straighten up. But the slouch is tempting still. My parents like to call me Zany, even though there is nothing zany about me. I am, in fact, very levelheaded.

Anyway, it's my dad onscreen. He knows I'm home and he has messaged me because he can't contain himself any longer.

So what do you think? Have you opened it? Do you love it?

That's when I notice the box on the desk. It's about the size of a handipak of tissues.

How great is that? he says, and for my dad this is pretty excited.

I open it up and pull it apart, and though I don't know every in and out of the technology, I know one thing before he even says it, but he says it anyway.

Now you are total is how he puts it. *This is the gizmo that pulls it all together, that coordinates all of our communications into one little package so that we can be in touch with each other, with the entire intellectual and emotional universe, at every second of the day. You only have to THINK about talking to your dad, and — poof! — you will be talking to him. No more of this unwieldy, archaic, and frankly embarrassing arrangement where you have to be in your room to access the full power of your life. This is sizzling hot, right off the line, Zane, and you are one of the first to have it anywhere. What do you say to all that?*

What do I say? I am staring at the gizmo in my hand, which is, in fact, called the Gizzard™, "the handheld that comes straight from the center of YOU!" With it comes a tiny wireless earpiece that looks and feels like a hunk of dark blue, well-cooked elbow macaroni.

You're speechless! Dad says.

When he whips out the exclamation marks, you really need to get out of his way. Anyhow, I figure the best way to agree is to remain speechless.

Good! Great! I am so glad I was able to be here to share this with you!

Only, he's not here with me. But he's not far-off, either. He is about as close as he gets, which is three doors down the hall in his study/office/zone/studio/contemplation station. I have heard it is a lovely place.

You just get yourself set up there while I go back to work. We'll talk later. See you, Zany.

I hit the seventh minute and my bladder tells me that, yet again, the wall knew just what it was talking about. I don't fight it. I do get tempted sometimes, out of pigheadedness. But really, I only embarrass myself.

I press the POWER button on the Gizzard™ and leave it there on the desk.

When I get back, I find it has programmed itself. It's instantly made itself a member of the team by nagging me.

Password? the little screen blinks at me. *Password? Password?*

Oh, but there is competition. My mother's afternoon televisual broadcast has just burst onto the scene. One of her specialty moves is the "In-Depth Celebrity Interview" with some uncelebrated celebrity who turns out to have no depth at all. She treats them very nice, though, because my mother is about the nicest hologram a kid could have.

I swing around in my desk chair to watch my mother, so I can have some material to include later when I write to her that she has done a good job.

Gizzard™ doesn't like to be ignored, apparently. It beeps. It beeps again. I turn and pick it up to find it has got *Password?* written all over its neurotic little face. It's in different fonts and sizes and colors and languages, and it is scrolling itself endlessly down the page.

"Sheesh," I say, and take it along with me as I wheel-walk myself in my desk chair, closer to my mother's interview. "And sheesh again," I say when I see who she is interviewing.

The Vet. Not a heroic war-scarred vet. Our vet, Dr. Gristle. He works on our many pets. In fairness, he is probably as celebrated as a vet can get, since he is a sort of snob society doc who makes you wait a month and a half to get shots unless you happen to be a successful Newsmama who can tell the world how fascinating and brilliant he is. It was one of his appearances with my mother that got him "discovered" by the government. They decided the good doctor was onto something with his electro-animal antics. They were right — he *is* onto something. And up to something, and behind something as well.

While to me this is the stuff of nightmares, somebody

big decided Dr. Gristle was the future, and made him Superundersecretary of State for Animal Bothering and General Creepy Weirdness. I think that's his title. What I know is that he is a regular vet the same way the CIA is just another phone service provider.

We saw him just the other day, as it happens, to get some kind of microchip shot into Hugo. It was the second time Hugo had been chipped by the guy, in addition to his annual vaccinations, so he doesn't seem to find him fascinating or brilliant at all. The first chip — known to most of the public as the Gristle chip, named by you-know-who after himself — was the universal that all pets get, carrying all their data, and code that allows us to control their basic movements from the central command system the way air traffic control does with planes. But this second chip — the Gristle 2.0 — is a kind of trial thing. Dr. Gristle asked if he could put it in, because it was part of his new big scheme for diagnosis and interactivity. The concept is that Hugo's own body system will communicate directly with his doctor down at the office, and every medical need will be anticipated by the system, with proper treatment planned before the pet's owners even know anything's gone goofy. Basically, Hugo will have a barometer just like mine. I might even know when he's about to precipitate, which would be helpful.

"So, you see, Cynthia," the big toothy vet is saying now to my mother and the world. "If my work is successful, we will have bridged one of the oldest and most vexing communication problems people face — having their animals *tell* them, in effect, when something is bothering them."

Dr. Gristle stares, all big faced and eager, right into the camera, like he is expecting an ear scratch and a crunchy treat.

Beep, is what the Gizzard™ has to say about it all. Beep, and beep, and beep. *Password? Password? Password . . .*

"Fine," I say, and establish my new all-controlling password without a second's thought. *H–U–G–O*, I type.

Gizzard™ kicks into gear, starts computing, controlling, and settling itself into the team. It's like Room and Speaker have just made a new friend. Now they can all talk about me.

Hugo comes trotting in, sits beside me, and stares. He's a white hodgepodge of terrier, with a thick, little body and a round, wide, whiskery face. It's like an eclipse of everything in the room when he goes into full stare on me. His face is Westie, though there is some bristly schnauzer floating around in there, and midget Yorkshire and some stout puggish something to boot. No two of his legs are the same length. . . .

"I hate it when you do that," I say, brushing him away. "It's like you're trying to force a confession out of me."

I turn back to the interview.

". . . and it will lead us out of the dark ages of interspecies misunderstanding," Dr. Gristle says. He is getting very worked up, gesturing toward the sky for some reason, then pointing at the viewers at home, almost jumping out of his chair. "The day will come soon when any pet that does not have The Gristle 2.0 communicator chip inside him will in effect be exiled by his owners to a place of darkness where he cannot be reached by anyone, a cyber no-man's-land, sentenced to Cyberia, if you will. But *with* my chip in there . . ."

Gizzard™ beeps at me, and I look down.

Where is this wonderful Cyberia? Can we go there?

I stare at the message. I look around the room.

Dad? I type.

No answer. I look around again. Up at the screen, where Dr. Gristle is getting further and further animated, while my mother tries to keep him in the chair. I look down at Hugo, who is not staring at me now but instead is watching the show.

Beep.

Doctor Fathead Vet Jerk. I really wish I'd chewed his fingers off when I had the chance.

That doesn't sound at all like my father. Or something the Gizzard™ would say on its own.

A double chill runs through me, down my spine and up again, as I stare at the most powerful man in veterinary medicine up on the big screen, then look down and over at my dog.

Hugo is staring at me full-on again. His big, white,

hairy circle of a face is like the center of all energy now, and I am drawn to it completely.

Beep.

Now I can see why you don't like it when I stare at you. It looks pitiful. Cut it out.

I jump up out of my chair and head for the door. I pass the panel with my vital statistics and find my temperature is now 99, and my blood pressure could launch a satellite.

I rush through the door and slam it behind me. I lean with my back to the door and my dog — or whatever it is — on the other side. From the panting I am doing, you would think the positions were reversed.

Beep.

Humans have wanted to talk to the animals for thousands of years. You finally get your chance and you run and hide behind the door. Lame.

Fine, he's got a point, but I'm still frozen.

Beep.

Zane?

"He knows my name," I blurt.

What do I look like, a springer spaniel? I've lived here for four years — of course, *I know your name. You don't know mine, though.*

"That's ridiculous. Your name is Hugo."

There you go, pure human arrogance. That's the name you gave me. My real name, given to me by my own mother, is Narfuffnarfnuffn.

"This is crazy. This isn't happening, Narf . . . Nuffin . . ."

Call me Hugo. Now, get back in the room. We need to talk.

"But you can't talk — that's the point. Why is this happening to me now?"

I've always been able to talk. You just haven't been able to listen. Now we're hooked up. Isn't that great?

"I don't know. Is it? Is it great? I do know that you didn't scare me before, but you sure do now."

There is a pause. My dog has stopped talking to me. How should a person feel about that? Has anyone even said that before?

I stop leaning against the door, turn, and slowly open it a crack.

There it is. His big Hugo face practically blocking out his little Hugo body. It is so broad and round and white, he looks like a pie pan filled up with whipped cream. He is staring right up at me, tilting his head in the same questioning way he always used before he could actually question.

Beep.

Hiya, Zane.

This is the first time I have been able to put words to that look.

I have to laugh.

"Hiya, Hugo."

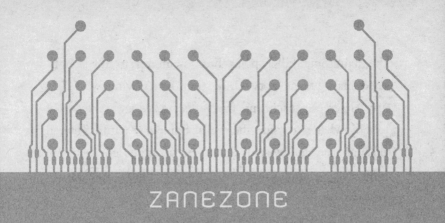

There is a great big indoor soccer field right in our sprawling housing complex, and on the other side of it is the indoor sports club, where I have swum and submitted to karate, archery, and other lessons all my life. Right beyond the indoor tennis courts, there's a small door that nobody ever uses. It leads outside, and with everything available indoors, very few people go outside. It's not that it isn't allowed. It's just not encouraged. All the facilities a sporto could want are inside, groomed and polished, and sharp. Outside is a great wide scruffy, unfocused space that most people find uninviting. Outside is a wild card. Outside is unmanaged, and unmanageable, which people around here don't much care for.

I like it.

A couple of years ago, Hugo and I tried out the door and found an old deserted path that goes about a mile into the woods. Locals love to be able to see the woods from the few windows of the sports center the way they love to see

the handsome killer polar bear swim up to the tough-
ened glass at the zoo. Only, they aren't windows. They
are telescreens, each and every one, relaying live feeds of
exactly what is outside the walls. Somehow nature filtered
through the audiovisual equipment is supposed to be an
improvement over the real nature that maybe might hurt
sensitive eyes.

But folks here have no desire to actually go into the
woods. Hugo, though, loves to walk this walk, and I love to
walk it. We both knew this long before we were ever able
to tell each other.

Beep. *I love it here, you know*, he barks.

"Yeah, I knew that."

More often than not, Hugo and I can do our entire
walk without seeing anybody else. The other people we pass
always have this guilty look on their faces. This is where
things slow down and smell better, where grass and trees
and birdsong take over from the bright lights and buzz of
the rest of life. I never feel switched on here, and that's a
good thing, even though I know a lot of people (especially
my parents) would hate it. I don't need to be tuned into anything here, and nothing is tuned into me.

Beep. *Want to throw the ball for m* —

"Grr."

That's me growling at the dog.

Problem?

"Problem, yes. What am I doing with this Gizzard™

thing, here? Why did I even bring it? This is what I don't want out here. You and I are supposed to be out walking, like always."

Beep. *But it's not like always, is it?*

"No. Because I am reading the stupid screen every five seconds. Because I am walking my dog and reading *messages* from my dog."

Maybe you should try that ear noodle thing.

"What? Right. Oh."

I pluck the small bendy earpiece off the side of the Gizzard™ and work it around in my ear, like I'm trying to make a mold of my hearing canal with chewing gum. It ends up fitting nicely.

"Say something," I tell Hugo.

"I think I need to go."

"Cool," I say. "This is so cool."

Hugo's voice is coming across clearly, smoothly, and, somehow, in a tone that is so suited to his Hugo face it's like the only possible voice he ever could have had. I've never heard a person from Yorkshire talk, never mind a Yorkshire-Scottish-German-schnauzer-pug-terrier, but I'm pretty sure this is it.

Of course, his first words aren't exactly for the history books. *I think I have to go.*

"Ah, Hugo."

He's got his little spine hunched, his tail pointing skyward.

"What did you expect?" he says, and his tone is none-too-pleased.

"I don't know . . . but . . . jeez."

I don't know what I expected. I don't know what *to* expect. Everything's changed now, isn't it? The whole nature of us, of our way together. It can't be the same, can it? I don't know what it can be, but it can't be the same, now that we can talk to each other. It's just too weird.

He is finished now and is staring at me. It looks very much like he is smiling as he does that little aggressive bull maneuver, scraping all his paws hard in the grass like he's wiping them off even though he hasn't stepped in anything.

I reluctantly take the plastic bag out of my back pocket. "Am I still supposed to pick that up? How is this supposed to work now? Am I . . ."

"I don't care if you pick it up or not. They're your fingers, I guess you can do what you want with them."

He jogs off happily toward the woodsy path while I take care of business and make a deposit in the appropriate bin.

"You know," I say, "all of a sudden that feels so degrading."

"I'd like to tell you I'd do the same for you, but I really don't think I would."

"What do we *do* now, Hugo? How do we move ahead? Everything is different now, everything is jumbled. This is . . . what *is* this?"

"This is what it always was. Only now you can understand."

"Except I don't understand at all. I can't treat you like a *pet*, can I? Not with you talking to me and all."

"Then treat me like a brother."

"You know, I never had a brother, but I'm pretty sure if I had to be his poop-caddy, the relationship would suffer."

"It was never my idea anyway. Scoop, don't scoop, whatever. I'm just the artist. If you can't appreciate my work . . ."

"Maybe I should go into the closet and get out the nice, simple robodog my parents gave me after you chewed up that shoe."

"That shoe looked at me funny. Anyway, just be patient and Doctor Fathead Vet Jerk is going to turn us all into robots eventually."

"What? He's not doing that. Why would he be doing that?"

"You're asking me? I don't know why you people do anything. All I know is, he's doing it. First he worked out the chip that lets you boss us in and out of the house when you want. Now he's developed the one that lets you read our hearts and minds. We've gone from being pets to being toys. Who knows how far down we can go from there?"

I come up on a tennis ball that some tennis doink must have released into the wild here. I pick it up.

"Just because you can talk, doesn't mean you know everything, Hugo. Dr. Gristle is a good vet. If he didn't give you shots, you probably wouldn't even be saying these things." I wind up and throw the ball for him along the path.

Hugo sits down, staring at me.

"What?"

"You're a sap."

"I am not a sap."

"You *are* a sap, and you have much to learn. Dogs are sharp judges of character — except, obviously, Irish setters. That vet of yours is messing with the way things work. Every time you take me to see him, I come back feeling a little less right. And if he's doing these things to me, the personal pooch of the royal family of glitz, I can only imagine what he's doing to the chumpy *lesser* animals."

Now he's freaking me out. First he starts talking to me, then he starts telling me conspiracy theories.

"Can't you just go fetch the ball?" I ask.

"I don't fetch."

"Since when?"

"Since I could tell you what I do and do not do. And while we're on the subject, you can just forget about *heel* and *beg*, too."

"Fine," I say. "I'll fetch it myself." I run right past Hugo and go for the ball. I think I threw it pretty straight and far, but when I emerge down the rougher end of the path out onto the soccer field, I can't find it.

I'm running in panicky little circles, trying to pick up a

glimpse of the ball, when Hugo catches up to me. He shows me up by finding the ball in the grass in about two sniffs, then dropping it at my feet.

"You're pretty good for somebody who doesn't fetch. Would you like to apply for the job of my dog? The position is suddenly vacant."

"Zane, you really should listen to me. This is serious."

"Look," I say, gesturing with the ball and talking a little too loudly for a guy who is having an argument with his dog in a public space, even if there's no one around. I lower my voice and start again. "Look, if my mother and my father and the veterinarian think something is good for you, then it probably is."

That settles that.

Only not for Hugo.

"It's not," he says. "It's wrong, it's rotten, and we need to do something."

"*We* need to do something?"

I swear, Hugo nods.

Right. I need to do something.

I throw the ball for myself again, in the direction of the home complex, and I run to catch it. Somebody's got to be the dog around here.

I'm bombing for it this time, watching the ball so I don't lose it. It bounces a few times, rolls toward the door we came through, and I track it down just before it scoots off the path.

But not before the white blur of Hugo shoots past me and scoops it up.

He is staring at me again, but this time with a tennis ball jammed in his gob. Good. He needs to shut up.

"I won't shut up about this, Zane. Something has to be done, and you need to help."

My turn to stare. He is there in front of me, ball in his little mouth, his beautiful round fluff of a face tilted sideways at that old familiar daffy questioning angle, and it is perfect. He is a dog. He is a great and simple dog, and I love him just like that.

"You are a *dog*," I snap at him, pointing harshly. Then I turn and head back inside the complex.

He is on my heels, but I don't care. I don't look and I don't listen. When we get back home, I burst through the back door and head down the hall for the door I could not wait to get away from just a while ago. My nameplate that's calling me in.

"I am with you, Zane."

I am coming, Room.

I open the door and — blip and bleep — the whole place is lighting up for me.

This is where I belong. This makes sense. My room is telling me what to do, and when to do it, and who I am.

"Thank you, Room," I say, throwing myself into the chair in front of my old computer, smacking the Gizzard™ down on the desk. Hugo has followed and is sitting next to me like usual, but I don't have to pay attention if I don't want to.

"You are welcome, Zane," Speaker says above me. "And you are hyperventilating."

"I was running. Don't worry about it."

"Running? There is nothing scheduled today that should have you running."

"Take a break, Room," I say.

I call up an essay I am working on for English, even though it is not due for a week. I like English. The rules never change.

There is a Yorkshire accent in my ear. "Talk to me."

I pull the noodle earpiece out of my ear and smack it down on the desk.

Back to English.

Zane, it says on my screen. My work screen. My old-fashioned familiar dependable never-changing chunky computer screen. How did he get in there? He didn't. He can't. This is not possible, and because it is not possible it proves I am just getting a little silly.

Silly or not, this dog is leaving.

I grab Hugo by his collar, and I guess I do it rough. He squeals, like a cry, and I let go. "I'm sorry, guy," I say, and touch his face. He leans into my hand, like he does, and fixes me with the eyes. "But you have to go," I say, scooping him up in my arms and putting him out into the hall.

I turn around, take stock. This is my room. As I know

it. The ZaneZone. Where everything talks but nothing is alive. As it should be.

My personal data panel is looking good. Temperature: perfect. Glucose, cholesterol, blood pressure: everything looking about right. My screens on the wall are showing me the world news and entertainment, which look exactly the same as they did yesterday. The dedicated dad panel is playing a rolling recap of my father's programs for the past month in case I missed anything, which I didn't. That Voice is in fine voice. I think he just waved at me.

I've got no talking animals. Hey.

It was my father's doing. It was a joke. It was him and the Gizzard™, and that's part of its "charm." The unit has a sense of humor (while my father, really, does not). That's what it was all about. That's what was happening.

The whole thing was probably captured on video. Ugh. It'll probably start playing on one of my screens any minute. Ah, what a dope, talking dogs . . .

It would have been nice, though. I probably couldn't pick a better friend or brother than Hugo to talk to.

My attention is pulled away by a squall of activity on a screen high on the wall. My cat, Sunflower (not my choice of name), has been hunting in the backyard, and the killer-catcam has picked up the motion. It's a lot of motion. He's got his sharpies into something substantial, and he's making a party of it.

He overcompensates for his name, but that doesn't excuse him for being a jerk.

I barrel out of the room, hurdle Hugo outside the door, and make it down the hall in Olympic hall–dash time. I'm out there and on the cat just as the action gets critical. Sunflower has the guy by the side of the neck and is giving it the jerk jerk.

It's a very cute mole. Who could maul a mole? I smack the cat on the hip, startling him, and scoop up the dazed and squiggling gray victim.

His fur is soft as rose petals, but a lot thicker and warmer. I cup him in both my hands — he's exactly that small — and ambulance him into the house. Sunflower, a very nervy creature under any circumstances, tries to come with us until I kick wildly at him.

The mole is either calming down or dying as I lay him gently on my bed. His little chest is still thrumping like a dwarfy speedbag, but he's no longer thrashing like crazy. I check him all over for blood and punctures and slices, Sunflower's usual bag of tricks, but I don't find anything obvious.

Hugo has taken advantage of the crisis to let himself back into the room. For a terrier, he possesses surprisingly little killer impulse, so he's not a worry here. In fact, there's something oddly nurse-y about his presence at such times.

He follows me around as I get a shoe box from the

closet and set it up as a bed, with a padding of tissues and a couple of thick white socks. I lay the mole in there and, again, I can't tell if he's relaxing or expiring, but I put my finger on his chest and feel warmth and rhythm in there. I pull one of the socks over him, up to his bitty shoulder things, and though he doesn't seem to notice one way or another, I think it's doing him good. I lie on the bed with the box next to me for I don't know how long, just watching, watching him, while Nurse Hugo sits bedside, doing the same to me.

Hugo looks like he wants to say something, but I don't want to hear it.

I know it's only going to lead to more trouble.

THE WILDWOOD

I feel something funny. At my foot, at my ankle. It tickles a little bit. I might be dreaming, or half-dreaming since I am only half-awake. Actually, probably only one-quarter awake. It's like a tugging, a fuzzy rubbing, then a tugging. It's not the worst sensation to wake up to, warm and attentive and kind of playful.

I'm sure it's a dream. I fall back asleep.

No. This isn't right. Things are not the way they are supposed to be. I jump up in my bed and look all around, feeling strange and foreign and lost. This is not how I wake up normally. When I wake up, my world wakes up around me, and everything is so orderly you would be certain this is how the world has always been. As I said, when I walk through my door, my room snaps to life, with all my devices tuning into my transmitter. The same thing happens when I wake up, since, just like Santa Claus, the central control system knows when I am sleeping, knows when I'm awake . . .

But nothing. I am wide awake, and there is nothing but silence in my room and, holy smokes, it is freaking me to mania. The telescreen monitors should be on, the voice should be intoning my day's schedule and telling me which socks my mother thinks I should put on to best defeat my athlete's foot. (Does nature bestow gag ailments to remind you of all the great things you are not? Athlete's foot on the unathletic likes of me? What's next, machine gunner's finger? Tap dancer's hip?) By now, I should be staring directly across the room at the most reliable and homey of our family morning rituals: The Breakfast Broadcast. With my parents' jobs requiring regular early mornings, I wake up every day to them already gone and my breakfast made and waiting for me — the video evidence of it projected right there onscreen, live and sizzling. And the aroma should be filling the room, piped in through the Scent-o-Com, to be sure I am pulled out of bed. The smell of bacon and maple and hot chocolate pumped into my bedroom — that does it every time.

But not this time. I have none of it, and I jump out of bed like I've been catapulted. I flap around feeling lost and weightless, grounded to nothing.

Then I notice. I stop and I notice.

It's gone. From my ankle, my controller. Sender, receiver,

coördinator of all the information of my days. Center of my life. Is gone. All that remains is the wire that ran out of the unit and into me, under my skin, into my bone marrow and beyond. It's just sticking out there, just above my ankle, chewed, frayed away. Funny it never struck me as odd when the wire was plugged into the unit. But now that it's just running out of me, like I'm a disconnected machine, it gives me a shiver and I look away quick.

I look beside the bed. The mole box is empty. I look beside the mole box. Hugo is sitting there staring at me.

Right. *Now* I want him to talk. "What's happening?" I plead. "What's going on? Where's my connection, Hugo? I need my connection."

He's not talking.

I run to my desk, pick up my Gizzard™, and switch it on. "Message me," I say desperately. To my dog.

Nothing's coming. Gizzard™ is working — it's displaying the temperature outside and the time and other useless information, but it's just a *thing* now, like any other thing. I put Gizzard™ back on the desk — still flashing stuff, but thanks for nothing — then grab the earpiece noodle and fit it in my ear, going back to my serene little Buddha of a dog and pleading with him, "Talk to me. I'm nowhere. I need to be somewhere."

When he does and says nothing, I rush out of my room and down the hall. Everything seems as it always seems, but the big difference is, it's all having nothing to do with me. Nothing in the house is talking to me; nothing is tuned to my frequency.

I get to the kitchen, and there is my breakfast, sitting warm under the heated glass, the hose of the Scent-o-Com hooked into it and trying its little heart out to pump essence of three cheese and tomato omelette to me in my room.

I run back to the ZaneZone, which isn't very Zane right now, and get myself dressed quickly. I don't know why I bother, since I don't know what to do or where to go, because nobody will tell me. Dressed, desperate, and clueless, I stand in the middle of my room, at the center of the scary silence, waiting for some kind of sign. Even a communiqué would do.

"Hugo, why would some mole want to steal my controller? Why would anybody have anything to gain from doing this to me, making me lost and disconnected from everything? I don't understand why, Hugo."

Hugo takes over and takes pity on the pitiful. He walks over and gently bites at my pant leg. He grabs, pulls. He pulls a little more, not the classic terrier pull with all that mad head shaking and snarling, but a guiding, easy tug.

What else am I going to do? I'm moving.

We leave the housing complex. We leave the safety of indoors. And then we go even farther and leave the path we always walk on. Hugo is leading me straight out into the WildArea, the place we're absolutely, positively, under-no-circumstances supposed to go. This isn't just trespassing — it's endangerment. But Hugo doesn't care. He keeps going. And I keep following. Because I need my transmitter back. And, I admit it, because I'm curious to see how wild the WildArea is.

At the start, there's a pond that nobody swims in and nobody skates on because it's famous for the field of vines that lives not far from the surface. The WildWater, everybody calls it. The vines pulled a few people under a long time ago and never gave them back. The pond's way of protecting its privacy, I guess.

The privacy is further taken care of by the WildWood, the dense thicket of woods that lies around and far beyond it. As I take my first cautious step inside, I wonder: How could I have forgotten this? Once, when I was six or seven, I ran away here. I didn't mean to run away — I was taking a rare walk outside with my sitter, and when she stopped to talk to a friend, I just set off. Suddenly, I was an explorer — wandering, digging, watching. All the plants and pests of this place were mine and I was theirs, and we all knew that. I couldn't have been gone longer than a few hours, but when they found me, I was pulled indoors for my own good for the rest of forever. How could I have forgotten this so completely? For those hours, it seemed like such a big part of me. Now it's coming back. My head is swimming with thoughts and senses, smells of all the green and water and wild garlic and a tiny bit of pleasant danger. This is where the physical me went, and it shivers me now to think how completely I lost it when I came indoors.

There are now the remains of paths that were once popular, long before I was born, and a narrow walkway circling the water all around. The city stopped taking care of them a long time ago to discourage people from getting too friendly with the unfriendly pond. Because despite the stern warnings posted and the convincing legend, there were always some jolly teenagers willing to have a picnic and a party down there and then somehow winding up emponded and needing rescuing. Nature has been allowed to take back the pond area so thoroughly, you could still have a picnic there, but it would have to be a party of one, and you'd have to do it standing up.

This is where Hugo leads me.

By the time we stop, my body is so crisscrossed with thorns and branches and possibly unseen claws, I feel like I've been dragged through a barbed-wire fence. As we penetrate deeper into the woods, each step brings us into more tightly packed, heavily armed nature. It's as if somebody is telling us, *If you want to come to this place, you'd better be serious*. We've traveled through acres of dense growth and stand not six feet from the edge of the homicidal water. Hugo, of course, is fine, looking like he just stepped out of a wash and blow-dry. And he's giving me the stare. The stare is mighty unhelpful right now.

"You know, we never talk anymore," I say to him. Whether he can talk or not, I know he gets sarcasm.

He stares.

"So, what's your *point*, Hugo?" Patience isn't an option now. Even in my own room, I was feeling lost and alien and in trouble, and now the jungle seems like it is growing thicker around me as I stand, threatening me maybe for forgetting about it all these years.

Hugo is standing with his back to the water, while I stand facing him with the woodland and the rest of the world behind me. All of a sudden, I see his point.

"Holy smokes," I say and back up unwisely into the foliage. I fall down hard, but hardly register, as the action at water's edge is about all I can take in.

Moving slowly but steadily up the bank toward us is what must be the world's largest terrapin. His shell is about the size of a manhole cover, and it looks just as heavy. He is missing one whole front leg, and the way he compensates is by using his head, thumping his sharp bullet beak right into the ground when it is the missing limb's turn to work. You would think this would make him look pitiful, but no, the effect somehow makes him look tough and far more intimidating than any turtle has a right to look.

He marches his way up toward us and parks himself

right next to Hugo, like they know each other. I am really crashing a party I don't even want to be at.

And the best part is: There, on the terrapin's remaining front leg, is my stolen controller unit.

"Right," I say, climbing back to my feet. "That's okay, Mr. Dinosaur Turtle, you can just keep that. This is all getting too much for me. Hugo, you can come, you can stay, your choice."

And no matter how scratchy it is, I start marching quickly back the way I came through the jungle.

I don't get far. Two strides in, I stop again to take in the scene before me. Animals are all over the place. Birds and mammals and reptiles of all kinds are filling the branches and undergrowth wherever I look. I have never seen this kind of variety in one place, and there is a good reason for that — they don't belong in one place. Squirrels and pigeons and blue jays — sure, they're native. But what explains the sudden wild world where a marmoset hangs out in a tree not two miles from my house? And a falcon? A chinchilla? And what's with the pony?

I'm not afraid — well, I am, but not as much as I could be. Because it's not like they are misbehaving. They are polite, and appear to be doing nothing more than waiting. For what? I don't know.

It's just the wrongness of the arrangement. How it's all not really supposed to work this way. That's what sets my feet tingling and turning me back toward my dog for enlightenment.

"Hugo?" I say, my hands spread out in pleading position.

Hugo makes a little snarffle noise into the ear of the terrapin. The terrapin comes toward me with that awkward but truly unsettling walk of his: foot-foot-face-foot, foot-foot-face-foot. It's like Hugo has sent his goon after me until the terrapin stops at my feet and, with some finesse, uses his mouth to pull the controller unit off his leg.

I waste no time. I am like a guy in a spy movie who's been trapped at the bottom of the ocean and is cut loose, thrashing for the surface and air and life.

I strap on the unit, then manage sloppily to twist its wires back onto the wire running out of me. As I do it, the connection crackles back to life, loud and buzzy. All at once, the wild world comes crashing into my head.

Voices — my goodness, such voices — screaming, squawking, all so loud, all so urgent and sure and mad, banging into my head, through my ear, through the earpiece noodle still so comfortably snuggled into my ear.

"WE DON'T WANT IT YOU GOTTA HELP HELP US YOU HAVE TO HELP DO IT DO IT STOP IT MAKE THEM STOP YOU HAVE TO HELP DO SOMETHING DO SOMETHING DO SOME-THING DO SOMETHING HELP US YOU HAVE TO HELP US YOU HAVE TO HELP ZANE ZANE ZANE . . ."

"Aahh," I shout, shake my head, slap at my ear to fight it off.

"Easy," says the familiar broad Yorkshire accent that pulls it all together, calms it all right down.

All the voices stop, and I am left with Hugo.

"Welcome to Cyberia," he says.

I don't know how to respond. The best I can do is say, "I see. It's a very nice place you have here. Thanks for showing it to me. Can we go home now, where things are a little more normal and my wall can tell me if I'm having some kind of brain seizure?"

"Look. I tried to tell you this was serious. We need some help."

I start looking all around again, trying to take in all the creatures individually. I notice my mole friend. Can't help but think of all the great times we had, me and ol' Mole. Thieving, dirtbag, ol' Mole.

"So, is it like a club or something?"

I simultaneously hear a barrage of two sets of noises. Their squawks and roars in the air, and their desperate voices in my head.

"Yeah, it's a club, and you're in it. That's why you're going to help us."

"Hey, Hugo," I say, gesturing all around, "nothing personal, but I don't see how I could belong to this . . ."

"You're caged like the rest of us, Zane, and you know it.

That's why you've been chosen. Because you are caged, and at one time you weren't, and you understand us."

I perk up at the sound of it. "Really? I've been *chosen*. I'm very *flattered*. But here's the thing: I'm not in any cage, and, as a matter of fact, neither are you, Hugo. You have a pretty nice life, you're welcome very much. And so do I. So I'm going back to it right now."

This time, I mean it. I turn and tear through the woods, scratching the life out of my arms and legs as I go. I jump over small animals, zag around bigger ones, duck flying and jumping creatures, and somehow I get my Zany self (yes, I am suffering temporary inZanity now) out of the area and back to the housing complex and my home.

Home, house, room. The ZaneZone never looked so good to me. I need the world I know, the world that knows me. Who wouldn't feel the same?

I brush my fingers over the friendly, reassuring old ZANE sign on my door, then I let myself in.

But what do I let myself in for?

As I step in, as usual, my room wakes up, lights up, fires up. Everything kicks in and calls out, and, for a small portion of a fraction of a second, I am filled with comfort and joy. But it is over just as quickly.

My room is going mental.

There's a problem. There's a problem. There's a problem. Zane? There is a problem. . . . The sound is louder and higher than I have ever heard it. The screens are lighting and flashing images so fast I can't make anything out. It looks and sounds like a panic attack. *The gap! The gap is unexplained and unacceptable. This cannot happen.*

I have my eyes shut and my ears covered because the sensory bombardment is total. "Cut it out, Room," I shout.

Time unaccounted for, Zane! There was no wake-up. You cannot appear from the outside if you have not first woken up in bed. You cannot come in the door if you have not gone out the door.

"Stop it," I say, and with every second I am growing more agitated. It's irrational, I know, but I am getting the urge to *fight* my room. I want to punch my room. It has a punchable personality right now, but no punchable face, and that fact is just making me angrier. "You do not need to know everything about me, Room."

Yes, we do. Yes, we do.

"Room, you're really starting to get up my nose. A guy does not want his room up his nose."

Parents must be notified.

"No," I shout. "No, parents must not —"

Parents notified.

"You are such a jerk —"

Beep.

Gizzard™ would like a word. It's a little excited over there on the desk.

Beep. Beep. Vibrrrrate . . . vibrrrraaate . . . .

"Hi, Dad."

"What's happening over there? What's going on? I don't understand, what's this gap about? How could this happen?"

My mother's oversize but perfectly groomed head pops up onscreen on the wall. "You haven't even touched your breakfast, Zane. It's well past breakfast. I don't understand."

My glucose level is low. So says my wall.

Hugo's voice is in my ear noodle. "You going to open up and let me in?"

I rush to the door and throw it open.

"You were right. You were right. I do live in a cage."

"Of course I was right. Never argue with a Yorkshireman."

FRIEND

"So, you see."

Hugo knows very well I don't see a thing. I have my face pressed hard enough into my bed that if I lifted my head you would find an imprint of my mug in the mattress. But since I have no plans to ever lift my head again, no one will ever see it.

"No, Hugo, I don't see."

"Yes, you do. You see, you saw, and you can't go back now. You are in a cage like the rest of us — a different kind of cage, but a cage. And, like the rest of us, you want to get out."

"That's not true. I didn't mean it when I said that. My blood sugar was just low, and I needed a nap. My wall told me so. I had a nap. I'm better now. I'm refreshed. I'm sensible again."

I don't think it has slipped my dog's notice that I am saying all this into my mattress while I lie facedown and lifeless.

"You sound like more of a robot than your stupid room."

My stupid room joins the discussion at this point. "Hugo has an appointment," Speaker says.

"I do not," Hugo says. He's not talking to the wall — the wall can't understand him. He's saying it to me.

The wall goes on. "Three thirty this afternoon. You are to bring Hugo into Dr. Gristle's office."

I sit up. "He just had an appointment. He doesn't need another one."

"Hugo has an appointment. The doctor needs to see him."

"Oh, no," Hugo gasps.

"What? Hugo, what is it?"

"It's the chip. He's reading me. He's reading me right now and he doesn't like what he's seeing."

"Then the chip works. That's good."

"No, that's bad. There's nothing wrong with my health. It's my attitude that's gotten the good doctor's attention."

"It is time to go," Wall insists.

Wall may not have used the words *you've got no choice*, but — trust me — they were in there.

--●--

You know that thing where you're sitting in the vet's waiting room, and your dog stands there trembling and whimpering and generally embarrassing you? Well, we are in that waiting room, and my dog is being that embarrassing, but the twist is that now we can talk about it — as long as we're discreet.

"I didn't think dogs could be paranoid," I say.

"I am not paranoid. I am perceptive."

I am having trouble taking him seriously, with all the high-drama quaking and crying he's doing.

"See, I was expecting *brave*," I say. "That's what I thought dogs did. Brave, hungry, and loyal."

He switches now from simper to snarl. *Rrrrnn Rrrrnnn.*

Turns out, he's laughing. This is how he laughs, apparently. I always wondered why he growled when I made muscle poses in front of my mirror.

"What's so funny?"

"Loyal. I always love that. Your dog is about as loyal as your toaster. I wouldn't trust me as far as I could throw me, and without thumbs, that's not very far."

He's lying. I have to believe it's just nerves talking.

I'll give him this: It *is* a highly intimidating waiting room. People are coming and going at a pace that suggests pets are being processed by a race car pit crew in there. Half the pet owners are wearing some kind of uniform or other, and the rest look as if they should be wearing some kind of uniform or other. The dogs even look in uniform. Nobody walks, everybody marches. There are screens all around us playing the amazing pet tricks of the all-star Gristle clients.

A gray seal tugs a damaged cruise liner safely into port. A Doberman slam-dunks a basketball into a regulation height hoop over a whole college team. Across the top of the screen a condor suddenly appears, towing a long advertising banner printed with Dr. Gristle's demented face and his phone number. It's the only smile we see, until . . .

"Zane, Hugo, how are you boys?" Dr. Gristle says as he sweeps us into an examination room. He always does that, sweeps, like he's arriving on the set of his own television show. His manner, too, is like that, bubbly and bright and dazzling.

"Underneath," Hugo says, "he's pure evil."

I try to ignore this, even though I have to admit Dr. Gristle has always made me feel a little uneasy. "We're great," I tell him, "which is why I guess we're wondering what we are doing here."

He switches, just like that. He goes from happy-jolly to warm-concerned as if he's being cued.

"We are here," he says solemnly, "because I want nothing but the best for our pal Hugo here."

"The best? For me, he wants the best? Ask him why he's wired me up like a car alarm. Go on, ask him."

"What is wrong, exactly, with our pal Hugo here?"

"Well, I don't want to alarm you, but the readings I'm getting indicate some heart trouble."

"Heart trouble?!" Hugo chokes out.

"Heart trouble?!" I say.

"Heart trouble," Dr. Gristle confirms. "Don't be alarmed, Zane — it's still early . . . and manageable. It's a good thing he had the Gristle 2.0 chip in him, or who knows how long this might have gone undetected. Right now, I just want to run a few tests, then we can get him on some medication that will keep him calm and unstressed."

Hugo starts to back away. "He's on to us," he whispers.

"Don't be nuts," I tell him.

"Excuse me, Zane?" Dr. Gristle asks.

"Sorry, Dr. Gristle. I was just trying to get my dog to relax."

"Don't let him know, Zane. Don't let him know we can communicate, or he'll sedate both of us. He's evil."

"Don't be nuts, please."

Dr. Gristle looks at me skeptically. "You already told him that, Zane, and frankly I don't think it's having any effect. Why don't you let the professional handle the situation for now. Then, once we've got our course of action sorted, I'll implant one more chip into Hugo."

"Right. I'll be a whole bag of chips!"

"Why another chip?"

"You are an inquisitive young fellow, aren't you, Zane?"

He tousles my hair. Ever have that done to you? It *is* very close to evil.

Hugo sounds scared.

"I don't want another chip, Zane," he says.

"What's the chip for, Doctor?"

"We'll get to that later, Zane. Right now, I'm going to give this pooch a thorough going-over. I'm going to give him a mild sedative, since he tried to bite my fingers off last time."

"He even tastes like a jerk. Evil jerk flavor."

Despite the insider information I am getting from the patient, I don't think I'm really in a position to overrule the veterinary professional. I have to let him do his vetting. Especially when two rather large nurses come out to help him hold Hugo still. It's like they've been waiting the whole time to do this.

"I hate you," Hugo says to me as the needle penetrates his rump hump. "I've always hated you. All that tail wagging was just for show and meat scraps."

"I'm going to leave him with you while he relaxes. We need to check on another patient," Dr. Gristle says, heading out the door.

Hugo relaxes pretty quickly.

"You're my best friend, Zaneo," he says, slumping, his big moon face bumping flat into my chest. "I love ya, ya big, hairless dope. Gimme a kiss."

"You're talking nonsense now."

"Oh, you wanna fight? You wanna fight me? Sweet. I've been waiting for this for a long time. Bring it on."

"Yeesh, Hugo, will you and your sedative calm down

for a minute, so you can tell me what you want to do about all this?"

His speech is slowing by the second. "What ... I want ... to do?"

"Yes. What do you want to do?"

"Run," he says. Then he starts to snore.

"Run," I say. "Great." I scoop up my dog — who's a lot heavier than you might think, because of his big head — and bolt from the examining room. I head down the hall toward the exit — but then I see Dr. Gristle emerging from another room with a woman and a fat cat. He's swamping them with out-the-door reminders about fat cats and heart attacks, so I run the other way and shoot into an unmarked door at the end of the hallway.

As soon as I get in there, it starts.

"Come on, Boss, let me out. Be a good boy. I'll be your friend. Help. LET ME OUT. LET ME OUT. LET ME OUT. I didn't do nothing. HE'S KILLING ME. He's gonna kill me. I'm already dead. I'm going to be a mother. A mother shouldn't be behind bars. Please? Please? Please? You smell like a nice kid. Please?"

Probably forty cages, varying shapes and sizes, are stacked on top of each other like milk crates, and nearly every one holds a prisoner. Big cats and small dogs and birds and reptiles and you name it, and they all want out and they all want me to know it.

"I can't just let you all out," I say.

"Ah, you understand us," says a fluffy white Persian cat who looks like my mother. "You are Our Friend. I knew you were Our Friend. I knew you would come for us."

There's no way these could be the same animals who were out in the woods a couple of hours ago. Word's traveled fast — and I have no idea how.

"What do you mean?" I ask. "How do you know about me?"

"The mole told us."

The mole! This is how he repays me for saving him!

"That mole really needs to mind his own business," I say.

It's the cat who answers. "I will tell him that," she says, "just as soon as you let us out of here."

Heavy Hugo is starting to pull my arm out of its socket. I lay him on the floor in front of the cage wall.

"Why are you carrying around a dead dog, Friend?"

"Right, first, don't call me Friend. I am Zane, and I don't know you enough to be your friend. Second, he's not dead; the doctor just sedated him."

"Well, that's not good." I can't even tell which animal is telling me this.

"It's nothing serious."

"Heart trouble?" This one comes from one of the dogs in the back.

"Yes . . . how did you know that?"

The dog, a deep-voiced Labrador retriever, says, "Let's

just say we've all been there. Please, just unlatch these cages."

"Listen, I understand. Nobody likes being in the hospital. But I'm sure you all have nice families waiting to collect you and then everything will be fine."

Several of the animals answer at once.

"We have no families."

"So where do you live?"

More voices join in. "Here."

"Why do you live here?"

The cat gives me a look that's so sad I almost have to turn away. In a grave voice, she tells me, "We're here so the master can invent things for his masters. He writes books and goes televisual while they rule the world and we become robopets and cuddly spies, weapons of quiet destruction on little cat feet."

"Wait — what do you mean, rule the world?"

"Quiet now! He's coming."

"What? I don't hear anything. What makes you think . . . ?"

"I'm a cat, for goodness sake."

"I have to hide."

A new voice calls out, "Here."

Down at the end of the line, on the bottom row where the big cages are, a big hairy chow is gesturing for me. I pick Hugo back up, dive down there, and slip into the empty cage on the far side of the chow. He blocks a lot of the view, and when I flip Hugo onto my back, I could be just another sleeping dog or a fireside rug.

The door opens, and I hear footsteps.

"Hmmm," Dr. Gristle says, addressing the gang. "This is strange. I don't suppose any of you saw a weedy young lad with bird's nest hair and a pan-terrier thing with a freakishly big face?"

Grrr. Hugo is waking up. *Grrr.* I can feel his growl more than I hear it. And he wasn't even called weedy.

"No, of course you can't tell me, can you?" Dr. Gristle's shoes click on the tiled floor as he paces back and forth in front of the assembled incarcerated crowd. "How I wish you could, though. Wouldn't that be wonderful?"

I am busy keeping myself flattened to the floor, but I allow my eyeballs to follow him as much as they can. He kneels down a couple of cages away from me and puts his fingers through the mesh of a cage to scratch the white fur of whatever is in there. He is nodding away as he scratches, nodding and talking and scratching with the animals.

"I would love for you to talk to me," he says sadly. "I would love to know what you're thinking, to know what you all are feeling. We'd all be great pals then, wouldn't we? If everybody could just understand everybody . . . we'd be great pals, wouldn't we?"

It goes quiet as he looks everybody over. Waiting for a response? Hoping?

This is our evil doctor?

"Well," he says, pulling away, "if I can't get you to talk, there are other ways to find out what we need to know."

After another quiet, almost expectant minute, the doctor leaves. Hugo revives on top of me.

"See, what did I tell you?"

"See, nothing," I say. "He talks like he's the nicest guy in the world."

We hear banging and slamming all over the offices, then feet stomping down the hall toward us. The door swings open, and we go flat again. Dr. Gristle storms back into the room with the two burly nurses as backup. He rushes toward a cage containing a baldish, trembling Pekingese-like mutt.

"Well, our mongrel friend seems to have vanished," Gristle growls. "So I guess *you'll* have to take his medicine for him." He opens the cage and snags the Pekingese by the scruff. He marches out the door, swinging the dog along like a whimpering, squirming handbag. The scowling nurses follow. Their steps are almost military in precision.

"What's he doing?" I whisper.

"He's nuts — *that's* what he's doing," Hugo says.

Hugo climbs off me, and I sit up in my cage. It's a tight squeeze, with my head pressed to the top of the cage and the sides feeling like I'm being wrung out in cheesecloth. Very uncomfortable. "He can't do that. That poor little dog. What's going to happen now?"

"He's going to get *improved*," says our cellmate, the chow.

Hugo stares at him. "Is that why your tongue is blue? It was that evil doctor, wasn't it?"

The cage is really bothering me now. It's getting at me, and I'm having trouble thinking about anything else. Like wearing a shirt full of hair after a haircut, then having somebody sit on your chest and pin your arms down. It's maddening.

I burst out of the cage so fast I bang into the wall opposite it. Then I stand right back up and address the other prisoners.

"Cages," I say breathlessly, "really stink."

I am blasted with a wall of sound as every creature in the place violently agrees with me and badgers me into letting them out.

"But how can I do that?" I plead. "I'll get in trouble. He'll know it's me. He knows my parents. Where would you even go?"

The fluffy white Persian who looks like my mother also serves the same function in their world that my mother does in mine: She's the spokesperson for everybody.

"We'll go with you, Friend."

"Stop calling me Friend! I don't deserve it!"

Her eyes are big and round and bright as lemons as she looks at me, sad and intense. Then the whole bank of them become one big, soft, wet wave of sad eyes, trapped and scared and needy eyes, and I don't have anything like the strength for this.

Hugo, the only other free-range creature here besides myself, rams my knee with his big melon head. I look down at him; he looks up at me.

"Aw, go on, Friend."

The place goes a little nuts again. In my free ear, I hear a bunch of animals in cages barking and yeowling and squawking. At the same time, in my ear noodle, I hear the chant, *Friend, Friend, Friend, Friend* . . .

"Ahhh," I say, and run along the line of cages, snapping off the latches one by one and flipping open the doors.

"Okay," I say when they are all out of the cages and climbing over one another to get to the door. It's like a barnyard pileup; nobody has any patience, and I'm flattened to the door. "Listen up! Follow me and stay quiet. I have a place. But we have to get out of here first, and that's the hard part." I listen at the door, but there's not a sound.

"He's in the exam room," says a deep voice with an oldworldy accent. There is a bat on my head.

"Is he really?" I say, trying not to freak out because *there is a bat on my head.*

"Yes. He just told the dog that it wouldn't hurt a bit."

"Cool, let's go."

I lead them out the door, then head down the hall toward the entrance. I can feel the breath of twenty different beasties hot on my neck, as suddenly the door to the exam room starts creaking open.

As their leader, it is my job to think quick and deliver.

I freeze.

Hugo bites my hand — too hard — and changes the team's direction.

"This way, Two Legs," he says.

The group has reversed and is heading like one big snake out the back way. I am no longer leading, but am, in fact, bringing up the very rear of the operation.

Once we all tumble out the back door and shut it behind us, we are here. Here we are. And here is . . .

"Where are we?" I ask.

"Walkies," Hugo says. "The exercise yard."

It is not a yard of any kind. It's an empty lot. An eight-foot-by-eight-foot concrete enclosure with a seven-foot-high wooden fence all around it. You couldn't get much exercise in here even if you had the place to yourself, and right now it is packed with enough ingredients for the world's biggest mixed-creature gumbo. If somebody hoses in some soup stock, people with bowls will line up around the block.

"What do we do now?" I ask.

"Throw me over," Hugo says.

"What? I'm not going to throw you over a fence."

"Right, then. I guess we're all going to die right here in the concrete death garden."

While Hugo and I debate just how we are going to go

about saving the entire animal kingdom, a portion of it wisely decides to save itself. Five cats, one ferret, and one skinny iguana scurry up and over the fence and are gone like smoke. Two white rats squeeze through a low fence crack no bigger than a Junior Mint. It gives me the shakes when they do that.

I am left in the yard with a variety of dogs and one runty potbellied pig the size of a football. None of them has any chance of getting over or under that fence. With my level of fitness, I'm no sure thing to make it over myself.

An alarm starts to sound. It's loud. Very loud.

"I'm sorry, guys," I say. "I think I've let you down."

"That's okay, Friend," says the chow. "Thanks for trying."

Dr. Gristle busts out into the yard.

"What are you *doing*?" he demands. He's trying to stay calm, but there's murder in his eyes.

"Exercising," Hugo says to me. "You're exercising us. Everybody, mill about in an orderly, energetic fashion."

"I'm exercising them, Doctor," I say like a dog's dummy. All around me the dogs and pig flow into a spontaneous exercircle, walking around and around me like I am the center of a merry-go-round.

Dr. Gristle is very impressed or shocked or something because all he can do is stand there gape-mouthed for a minute as the team maintains its uncommon discipline and pace without any apparent human input.

"This is so beautiful," Dr. Gristle says. He keeps walking up to each dog (or pig) who passes, reaching out like he's going to touch, then backing away as if afraid to break a spell. "This is amazing. They are special for you, aren't they? You are special."

The animals keep on parading around me, and the doctor gets ever more excited.

"How do you get them to do that for you, Zane? I've been working on . . . I've been trying forever to get this kind of responsiveness, with very limited success."

"It's because we hate him," Hugo points out.

"What is your secret? Please . . . ?"

"No," Hugo warns. "Do not say a thing to him, Zane. Don't let him know we are talking to you, or it will be bad for everybody."

"I don't know, Dr. Gristle. I brought them out here to the exercise yard . . . they started exercising. I guess they knew where they were and what they were supposed to be doing. Maybe they're just really, really clever."

"Oh, they are not," he says firmly.

Just then, every one of the circling animals stops still. They don't look at me, they don't look at him, they just stand there, each one staring at the back of the one in front of them.

He's rattled, eyes darting all over the place from animal to animal to me to the door behind him, back to me. "What's happened?" he asks. "Why did they stop?"

"How do I know? Maybe you hurt their feelings."

"They don't have feelings. Not that kind, anyway."

And just like that, they start again, parading in their eerie circle.

Now it's deep, like they are hypnotizing him or scaring the pants off him. He has lost some of that confident force he always has, that sense that he knows more than everybody else around. I like this, but at the same time find it a little chilling.

"Zane, what are you doing here anyway?" Dr. Gristle says as he zones on the marching animals. "You and Hugo were supposed to be —"

I need to make up an excuse, and fast.

"I heard some whimpering coming from that room, Doctor," I tell him. "I'm sorry about that, but that's just how I am. When I hear an animal in distress, I just have to go there. And they looked to me like they needed some fresh air and exercise."

"Well, yes. But there is no —"

Flattery. Got to charge up the flattery battery.

"And I knew, you being a big animal guy yourself, king of the animals, really — I saw you on my mom's program, by the way, and you were awesome — I figured you would feel the same way I did and you would want me to take them out."

"Yes, well . . . king of the animals? Was it good? Did I look and sound like myself, because I hear all the time that your voice and your appearance are distorted when you are on the screen . . . but you think it went well?"

Hugo mumbles, "You'd have to scratch my belly for a month to get me to roll like this."

I try to ignore him.

"Oh, yeah," I say, "everybody's going to want to come to you with their pets now. Hugo even *wanted* me to make an appointment after that."

"If you don't stop, I'm going to puke."

"Well," the good doctor says, tearing his eyes away from the hypnotic dog-pig roundabout. "Indeed. I — I suppose I'd better check on those other little pals of mine. They are my special charges, after all."

"After all," I say, and give him a thumbs-up as he heads to the empty cages. The minute he realizes that it's not only the dogs and pig who are missing, flattery will get me nowhere.

"What now, wise Friend?" Hugo asks.

"You'd better go," the chow says. "Over the fence."

"Yeah," Hugo says. "Let's get out of here. Hike me over the fence and let's scram."

"You can't just drop over like that," I say. "You'll get hurt."

"No, trust me, it's the only way I am just like a cat. Always land on my feet. Come on."

Gristle is back at the door. "Where are all my animals?" he shouts. He doesn't sound hypnotized at all now. Nope, not at all. The nurse-soldiers are behind him, looking ready to wrestle.

All at once, the remaining dogs and the pig rush him to stall for time. They are barking and yelping and jumping at him.

I heave the allegedly catlike Hugo over the fence.

"Yeoooww," he cries, and it sounds nothing like a cat.

I hop up and over with about the same grace, also screaming, "Yeoooww."

"Keep running!" Hugo yells.

Scratching, scratching, tapping on one of the telescreen monitors.

"What?" I say, rubbing one eye open as I gaze up. Because I have bounced up out of bed, my room is blipping and bleeping to life, so once again I have the electronic world harping at me from behind and nature's bounty nagging me head-on from my one electronic portal to the world right outside our home.

"Where are we supposed to go?"

"We don't know what to do."

"We're hungry."

"We're nervous."

It's the gang. The liberated felines and reptiles from Dr. Gristle's office, all gathered outside my house, speaking to the cam.

"Go where you want to," I say, opening the intercom for that monitor. "Do what you want to. You are free."

"Go where we want to?" They start looking around them, up, down, and sideways, at one another, then at me. "Okay, then," the cat who looks like my mother says, "we want to come in there. Let us in, please."

"Huh? No, you can't come in here. This house is filled already with pets. I can't suddenly roll in a bunch more. What would my parents say? What if Dr. Gristle found out you were here?"

"Him? He doesn't scare you. You're Our Friend."

All at once, her gang starts up behind her, "Friend, Friend, Friend, Friend . . ."

"Hey," Hugo says from the floor behind me, "they caught on pretty quickly to that buttering-up thing, didn't they?"

"Yes, and you can all just be quiet now."

"No," the cat says, "please, you have to help us."

I hear my mother's voice behind me and turn to see her face lighting up my wall. She is reporting a break-in and theft at a certain important animal research facility.

"I like her face," says the cat who looks like my mother. "I feel like I could trust her."

The Scent-o-Com is filling my room with the aroma of sizzling pork products.

"And the missing animals are very important to the ongoing work of the well-known veterinary innovator and governmental advisor, Dr. Gary Gristle."

"Hey," the cat says, a little perked up, "she's talking about us. I didn't know we were all that newsworthy."

Hugo is making that snarly-snuffy noise I now recognize as laughter. "Hey," he says, "she's reporting on you. Your own mother is reporting your crimes to the world."

"Think we could have some of those sausages out here?" the cat says. "We're starving."

"Hold on," a slinky ferret cuts in. "I can smell those sausages from here. Don't they smell like somebody we know?"

The cat is not entirely moved. "I'm hungry. Don't be a wimp. We can feel bad tomorrow."

"Oh, this isn't good," I say. "This isn't good at all. You guys have to get away from the housing complex. If they find you with me, everybody's going to wonder why I'm suddenly the neighborhood cat rustler. What'll I tell them?"

"Where are we supposed to go?" more than one voice asks.

"Wait right there — I'll be out in a second."

"Okay," the cat says, giving me a feline grin. "We'll wait. And bring the sausages."

I get myself dressed and collect my waiting breakfast in a plastic bag. When Hugo and I come around to the side of the house, all the climbing beasties have made themselves scarce in the trees of the yard. They are really good, so that if you didn't know to look for them, you would think you were alone. But the smell of my breakfast brings them down on me like very hungry rain.

"Okay guys, okay," I say after feeding the masses with my eggs and banana and all. "Let's go."

It must look at best peculiar and probably hilarious to see me leading the procession out toward the WildWood, and I do get looks. I double-time it, as if passersby will forget seeing me do the pied piper thing as long as the image doesn't burn too long in the mind. Once we get past the fields and away from the housing complex, there are fewer people, and we're less of a sight. Without too much fanfare, we duck finally, safely into the forest.

"This is it?" asks Mother Cat.

"Yeah," I say. "Isn't it great?"

"I guess."

The thing is, it is. Every time I come back here now, I am that little bit much more aware of what a great green earth-scented place the WildWood is. You can smell the WildWater, even, and smell how clean it is, even if it's murderous with vines. And best of all, for these lost souls, it is even enclosed by leaves and branches. It is like pulling the outdoors indoors with you, keeping all that canopy shelter and protection without giving up any of the clean and open.

One and two at a time, the animals who already live here come along to nose up to the transplantees. There's a lot of sniffing going on. There is a lot of animal stuff going on, *prrr*ing and *grrr*ing and *skeeek*ing and *awk*ing, and it looks to me as weird and off-track as I must have looked out on the path leading the animals to freedom. In my ear noodle I hear it, the translation.

They are comparing notes. Half of the animals have escaped from captivity, half have wound up here by nature's chance, but what they all have in common is that this is what they want, and it is all they want. There is no thirst for revenge against their captors. There is just an agreement that this life here, like my own WildWood moment in childhood, feels pretty much like the way things should be. There is not a creature here who wants to trade it for captivity.

"No offense, dude," says the sloth, descending from the serious height of a mature cypress tree. Descending. Very slowly.

"Are you talking to me?" I ask after waiting for him a while.

"No. Talking to that guy who came with you."

"Me?" Hugo asks.

"Yeah. I mean, no offense to you, but you choose to live indoors with the comfort and oppression and the stupid rules where everybody really hates you even if you don't know it. Again, no offense — if that's the way you choose to *not* live your life, we won't hold that against you here."

He's still not halfway down the tree. He's talking so slowly I could climb up there and pat him on the head and be back down on the ground before he starts his next sentence. He is climbing straight down, with his head pointed toward earth, exaggerating further the very long black hair he is cultivating at the front of his head.

"And, you," he says to me, "you really think you are Our Friend, but you are not Our Friend, you are Our Nothing, and you should probably just go home and leave everybody alone. Stop telling me what to do. You don't own me. And don't be spying around in my tree."

"I'm not . . . I nev —"

"That's it," he says. "I don't have to deal with this. I'm going back up my tree, and everybody better just leave me alone."

Just then, all the animals start fleeing every which way, like somebody's just fired a gun to disperse the crowd. They fly, they run, they dive. I hear the splashes in the pond and hope these guys handle the water hazard a lot better than my kind ever did.

"What's going on?" I ask the only remaining other being, Hugo. He's giving me the big face, but not much else. "What's the deal, Hugo? Where'd everybody go?"

"Why are you asking your dog questions here in the middle of the woods, Zane?"

I basically throw my entire chicken self on top of my dog at the sound of Dr. Gristle's assured voice at my back.

"Hey, Doctor," I say in a happy-go-stupid voice that ain't fooling nobody. I wrestle Hugo around a bit on the ground, tousling his mane some to add authentic boy-dog joshiness. Even if I wasn't faking, Hugo is not that joshy kind of dog.

"Knock it off," he growls.

"Just taking my boy out for a good walk, Doctor," I say. "Having some fun, getting some air and exercise. With his heart and everything, really important, right?"

Dr. Gristle's air of being constantly in a state of auditioning for something is not with him now. There is nothing sunny about him here and now and he has, in fact, made the woods less light-filled than it was before.

"Where did my animals go, Zane?" he says.

"Your animals? Oh, your animals? You know that's weird, but I never thought of you as having your own animals. Is that a thing, in your business, that people only think of you as working on other folks' pets but never having your own animals at home? Do you have pets at home? Any roommates? Any pals? Do you like animals, Doctor?"

"The animals," he says flatly, "from my office."

The Goth Sloth spoke faster than this. And he was more fun.

"Oh, right, them. I heard my mother talking about them on the news. I don't know anyth —"

"So why does my tracker tell me they are here, Zane? Hmm? Why do the animals' chips tell the control center that the animals are all here? Zane?"

My head is really hot now. I am suddenly very curious

to know what my wall has to say about my temperature and blood sugar and stomach acid and —

"Zane?"

I am good under pressure. Sort of. Not really.

"Sorry, Dr. Gristle, what was the question again?"

"Zane, stop this. There are many more people than me interested in this situation. Bigger people, more important people. But here's the thing — they're not sensitive types like us. They wouldn't be nearly as concerned as we would be about the animals' well-being. Or yours, for that matter. So this is my last warning. Let's not trouble others with our troubles, lest our troubles multiply. I want you to tell me —"

Suddenly, he's got more pressing things on his mind. Well, on his head. A bristly brown bat comes swooping down googly as a knuckleball from a high branch behind the doctor and lands *bap* on his head. In seconds, he is good and tangled in Dr. Gristle's hair, and it is freaking the man out.

"I thought that was a myth," I say, "the thing with the hair tangling."

Dr. Gristle is not his articulate self, and cannot enlighten me on this point. He swats madly at his own head and makes a scaredy whine noise like an empty blender.

The bat is more helpful. "We're bats. We do what we feel like."

"Cool," I say.

"Not cool, not cool," Dr. Gristle says as a second and

third bat join the batpack and drive him flailing and wailing back the way he came, and out of my WildWood.

"You can't keep me away forever!" he cries before he goes.

"For now will do," Hugo replies.

"S-s-s-s-see that?" says a fat snake, tongue-flipping me at the ankle.

"See what?" I ask, stepping back. Even if he can communicate, he's a snake.

"You'd like more of that, wouldn't you?"

"I don't know — maybe if you'd tell me what *that* is, I'd ask for some more."

"That," Hugo breaks in, "is strength, control . . . power. You like power, don't you, Zane?"

"How would I know?"

"Well, then use your imagination. How'd you feel if you could have the ears of a bat, the eyes of a hawk, the strength of a bear, the stench of a skunk . . ."

"Way to sell there, Hugo."

"Hey, don't knock it — it's a power. The point is, you can have all that, because you have all of us. We're with you, and you are with us —"

"I control the animals!" I cry, trying it out.

As I say this, all creatures great and small begin migrating away from me in all directions.

"Now look what you did," Hugo says. "Let me make this simple for you. We've got your back, Zane. We can help you in many, many ways, and we need you to help us. We don't want to be chipped and controlled and changed from what we are. There is a fight that needs to be fought, and we can't do it without help. Help is you."

"Help is me?" I say breathlessly.

"Help is you," my dog says, letting his big face droop sadly to the woodsy ground.

"Wow," I say, "you guys are in big trouble."

He looks back up at me, doing his famous, sad head tilt.

"Yes, we are."

"There are things going on, all over the place, Zane, and we just don't know what's happening. Things are changing, animals are acting not like they really are, and we are all scared."

Hugo's making me scared. I can maybe get used to him joking around with me. But having him be so serious is unsettling. He can be a grim little guy once he gets going.

We are doing our old walk around the park. All the other animals are back in the WildWood, scattered far from Dr. Gristle's reach . . . at least, for now. It is nice out, sunny and crisp and perfect for an October morning. It's a long weekend because of Columbus Day, and I am in a mood to not think about a whole lot, and that always matched up well with a long slow tromp in the park with my dog.

Before.

"So," Hugo continues, "we have our work cut out for us, Zane."

"Yes, well, what's our work, exactly, Hugo?"

Hugo goes silent. He also stops walking, at a curious spot. We are at the outside edge of the park, where the long impressive hedgerow banks up against the streetside and the paved, antipark world.

"What's up?" I ask.

He stares into the hedge, like a hunting dog finding something to bother.

I stare at the spot and wait, until suddenly a bristly brambly low spot on the hedge slowly unfurls itself and rolls out at our feet.

"Hey, you're a hedgehog," I say.

"*This*," the hedgehog says to my dog in a scratchy and skeptical tone, "is Our Friend?"

"Best I could do," Hugo replies.

Hedgehog is looking back and forth, up and down. His movements are not quick, but they certainly are furtive. There is nobody or nothing around beyond soft sunshine and some falling leaves, but he's not impressed by that.

"Listen," he says, "I can't be out here long."

"Why not?" I ask.

"How many hedgehogs you ever actually seen?"

"A few."

"And may I ask you what kind of condition they were in?"

Visions of roadkill splat through my head.

"Uh . . . mostly croaked, now that you mention it."

"Precisely. So I will get to the point. I got a rat, at

the track. And this rat, he tells me there's a lot of awful stuff goin' on down there, at the track. Greyhounds doin' stuff, climbin' trees, runnin' up the sides of buildings and stuff . . . pure freak, you know what I mean?"

"Pure freak," Hugo says solemnly.

I'm still not getting it. "Pure freak, I guess. And what, you want me to go down and . . . de-freak the racetrack?"

"You, Our Friend?"

"So they tell me."

"Then *vaya con Dios.*"

And just like he unballed, my multilingual hedgehog pal balls right back up into the safety of his disguise. Pure hedge, if you didn't know better.

"Right," I say. Hugo and I stand there for a moment more. "That was weird. But I guess we have work to do."

"What *we*? You're flying solo here, Zane. You have to keep a low profile."

"We can do that." I assure him. There's no way I'm doing this without Hugo.

"Right. Can you see me blending in at the racetrack, lining up with all the other stringbeans at the gate?"

Hugo's legs are like hairy white cocktail sausages.

It's a funny image.

"Stop laughing at me, Zane. I mean it."

He's protesting, but he keeps walking with me to the bus stop.

"Good luck," he says, suddenly serious again.

I have a feeling I'll need it.

I find out pretty quickly greyhound racing is not one of your glamour sports. The track looks like a prisoner-of-war camp as I approach. It's a small circular structure that could have been an open-air factory that doesn't make anything anymore. It's surrounded by a parking lot, which has only a couple of cars in it right now, which is surrounded by a tall, rusted chain-link fence, which is topped off by a lighthearted menacing curlicue of razor wire.

What's with the razor wire? Can the supermutts really jump that high? Is the general population so dying to get into a place that looks like it'll never let you out again?

"What's with you?" a big fat guy barks at me. He has hairy hands and a bald head and looks like when he shaves he has to shave right up to his bottom eyelashes. Maybe the people bark here to make the dogs feel more at ease.

"I asked you somethin', kid. Do you talk, or will I just bop you on the head and see if you squeak? What are you doin' in here?"

I have, apparently, strayed into his protected zone. I'm about three feet inside the gate, but nowhere near the actual track.

A brown rat comes wriggling up confidently behind the guy. His coloring makes him look just like he's wearing a vest.

"Um," I say, and point at the rat.

The man looks down. I might as well have been telling him his socks didn't match — which, trust me, would *not* bother him.

"So?" he barks. "Tell me what you want, or get out. We've got a big race later on today, and I don't have time for kidding."

"Flattery," comes the rat's instruction in my ear noodle. He has a voice like a salesman. "He is human, after all."

"Barely," I say.

"What?" Woof.

"Tell him who your parents are. Tell him they might want to do a story."

I don't want to know how the rat has found out who my parents are; clearly, word travels fast in the animal kingdom.

But I can't think of a better plan. I tell him who my parents are. And I tell him they might want to do a story.

Okay, so I'm a rodent's ventriloquist's dummy now.

At first, the man seems more scared than impressed.

"Huh?" he grunts out. "No, listen, we was cleared. We didn't do none of that stuff and we got our license back, and so, no. Get outta here, kid."

Great, now he thinks I'm an undercover reporter trying to shut him down. What next, rat?

Of course, the rat's one step ahead of me.

"You're happy he was cleared," he instructs. "You love dogs. You love racing. You think he's a fine guy. He runs an amazing operation. The track should get some good press. Sport of kings, sort of. His name is Jo-Jo Dolan, and you are a big fan."

I slobber, doing exactly what the rat tells me to do, and the big man melts like a tub of butter thrown on a campfire. Jo-Jo's clearly not accustomed to good press and flattery, not to mention having his name known by a stranger who's not flashing a badge.

"If it were up to me," I gush, "Mom and Dad would talk about you *every single day* on their programs. I'm your *biggest fan* in *the whole wide greyhound-racing world.*"

At first, I'm a little worried I've gone too far. But quicker than you can say "shame for a worthy cause," I'm getting The Tour.

The Tour involves this: Cages. Cages and dungeons. Cages *in* dungeons. It's like the whole structure that encircles the track and lies under the spectator stands is dedicated to keeping the dogs penned up when they are not running forty-five miles an hour after a fake flying rabbit. It smells in these catacombs, like urine, mildly rotting meat, and mold. There is low yellow lighting that is more depressing than total darkness, and an eerie lack of sound.

There is some activity among the cages. A flunky comes to take a few dogs for a walk and puts a few others back. There is some kind of rotation of food service, to which my rat and several of his rat friends help themselves without so much as a yip from anyone.

And is Jo-Jo embarrassed by what I've found on his premises, like somebody with a dirty house and unannounced houseguests?

Not a chance.

"My castle," is about all he says through The Tour. And he says it about 150 times.

Eventually we are out of the enclosure and into light and air. It's much better than the cages, which isn't saying much. I guess if I was one of the greyhound running machines, I wouldn't mind escaping into an oval like this. The air is clear, the track is groomed to a degree Jo-Jo has probably never experienced himself, and it appears to anyone on the outside that nothing matters to the track workers but the care and pleasure of the resident dogs.

"Bring him over here," Jo-Jo calls to one of the dog walkers escorting a greyhound around the track. He heads over, and the first thing I notice is that the kid, not much older than me, has a face almost exactly like the dog he's handling. Except for the acne and the cigarette.

"His name is SureShot," Jo-Jo says.

"Cool job you have here, SureShot," I say to the kid.

"The dog," Jo-Jo says.

SureShot, when he gets to us, is a wonder dog. You can see all of the muscles under his skin, from his temples to his neck to his shoulders to his abs. I have seen pictures of these guys in action, and even seen a few civilian greyhounds up close, but it didn't cover this. His thighs alone should be able to win races. If he had fingers, he could lift weights and fight as a welterweight. He looks like he's got extra gas tanks packed into those thighs for that late-race afterburner blast, and now I think maybe that high fence *is* needed, because this dude could clear a normal fence on one leg.

He seemed agitated enough when they were walking him, but now that he is forced to come over and do a completely phony sports-page interview and stop traveling all together, he looks like those muscles and bones are wriggling to slip right out of that skin and get back to running. There is hardly any skin, anyway, so he just might manage it. I imagine seeing a muscle-bone dog running off to get away from here, jump that fence, run run run to his heart's content.

Suddenly, I hear his voice in my ear. He sounds like he just gulped down twelve gallons of coffee and is speaking from the top of a barreling roller coaster.

"I just want to run, okay. I just want to run. You don't need to talk to me. I am an athlete, you know, I run. I love to run and I am good at it. You take one race at a time, keep your eyes on the rabbit, and, like, run. I don't want to talk about the past. You know, you train hard and dedicate your-self to the job and give the best performance you can for the fans, and still people want to question you, to doubt you, to be negative and bring up all that stuff. I don't want to talk about the past. I just want to run, and people are gonna think what they're gonna think anyway, so I don't worry about all that stuff."

Wow.

"Watcha think?" Jo-Jo says proudly.

"Wow," I say.

"He's a stud, that boy, a true champion. Loves to run. Lives to run. He spreads a lot of joy, this boy. People love to see him, and he loves the show."

SureShot goes on. "It's hard work, pure and simple, nothing else. I gotta work hard to put food in that bowl, a roof over my head. You don't produce results . . . you gotta produce, you gotta run hard, no matter what it takes. Win-ning. Right? Winning, if you're not running to win you're not running hard."

SureShot begins straining at his leash. His eyes are mad things, half rolled up into his head, and his movements are all quirky-twitchy like he's got nonstop shocks running through his toned body.

"Runnin' for love, ol' SureShot," Jo-Jo says. "He's just runnin' for pure love of runnin'. Can't hold him back for nothin'. Go on, kid, get him goin'."

The kid doesn't have much choice but to get him goin', since the dog is clearly the stronger one, and he has definitely decided the interview is over. But as SureShot pulls away, every fiber of him straining in one direction and towing the kid, he turns his head and looks right at me. His eyes briefly pull down from the maniacal rollback they've been till now.

It's a look that grabs me, pulls me, right up to him and into him. It's a look so sad that I don't know any human being who could make it. I am certain he is about to say something, and I wait for it.

And I wait. Like that, he's turned back again, broken into a run, pulling the handler behind. I tap at my ear noodle, so sure he has something to say to me, but nothing's coming over.

"Finest athletes in the wide world of sports," Jo-Jo says as one strapping, agitated dog after another comes and goes. "I love 'em like they're my own babies."

I'm picturing a family of sleek animals, all with Jo-Jo's gray meaty face, running forty-five miles an hour in a pack.

"I think I have to go now," I say.

"When do you think your parents would want to talk to me?" he says anxiously. "Will they bring a lot of cameras?"

This is really embarrassing. I don't think even my school newspaper would be interested in what Jo-Jo's been saying. And that's saying a lot, since nobody in my school reads the school paper. The only edition I have ever seen with my own eyes was on the hindquarters of a papier-mâché rhinoceros in art class.

"I'll be sure to talk to my parents," I say. "I'll be in touch."

"Great," Jo-Jo says, and shakes my hand. His hand, and now my hand, smells like coconut foot sweat. He must be lightheaded with the new positive celebrity he will be achieving. I swear, he spins on his heel before he heads off to the bowels of the building or points beyond, and leaves me there on my lonesome ownsome right on the track.

It's kind of cool, actually, to be surrounded by banks and tiers of stands that could be people looking down on me and waiting to cheer me on as I do something amazingly athletic.

I can get it, the thrill of why people might want this, why dogs might even want this. (Or, at least, why people might want to get it through dogs.) I spin around and around, looking up in all directions, waving to the little people. I can hear them in my ears, I could almost swear it's real, as I break into a little trot around the dirt track, then a run, then a sprint.

This is all right. This is something almost worth breaking a sweat over, getting breathless over. There isn't even anybody here to watch, or any other competitors to get worked up about, and yet I am worked up. I want this. I want to win. I am running, as if there was something to run for. And it feels great.

Now I'm tired. It's hard, this fast running thing. The crowd is still loud, but it can't carry me through, and I grind to a halt when I come upon the rabbit.

It's not real, of course. It's the mechanical rabbit, mounted on a post on a track that runs along the inside rail. It's the thing that gets all the dogs excited enough to chase like crazies even though up close it doesn't look much more like a rabbit than I do. It's like bent-up wire hangers covered in knotted pink socks. And what kind of a rabbit runs at a level three feet above the turf? Frankly, I don't think greyhounds are the cleverest creatures in the kingdom.

The crowd noise now actually grows louder. This is real, I'm not imagining it. I turn toward the stands again, as if I'll find loads of paying customers suddenly filing in to cheer me on.

But that's not it. It's dogs.

Probably half the population of runners on the premises, from the cages and all around, are assembled and facing me from across the track. All are leashed, held by flunkies who are straining to hold back two, three, four dogs apiece as they all pull hard toward me with some almighty singular purpose and one almighty, heartbreaking voice.

If a whole stadium could cry with pain, the sound would be this. If you listened closely to the sound of all the fans at a baseball game and found they were wailing in pain when you thought they were cheering, the sound would be this.

They are talking, through my ear noodle, in words of some kind, but it is as if they are words from a foreign language, human but not English, but it does not even matter. Their voices have bypassed my ears, gone right by the ear noodle, skipped any deciphering system at all, and they are speaking to me, the very me of me at the center of myself, and I hear this as clearly as I have ever heard anything.

"Take us away," they say. "Please, free us."

I'm standing there, covered in goose bumps and sweaty, at the center of a racetrack at the very center of sadness. It is hard to even look at the skinny, drooping faces on these powerful creatures, never mind hear them.

I can't take them with me. How am I supposed to take all of them with me?

"What, you gonna just stand there?"

I look down to find a crow standing next to me. In fact, I barely have to look down at all, since he's the biggest crow I've seen.

"I don't know," I say to him. "I mean, of course I'm not going to just stand here."

"So, what then?"

"I don't know," I shout and while I shout I make that stupid arms-flapping lunge forward move people do when they are trying to scare birds off.

Nobody's scaring this bird off, least of all me.

"Is that your move?" Crow asks. "'Cause if that's the best you can do, I don't see you helping *nobody*, to be honest with you."

"Well, thanks for being honest with me, because I don't know what my move is. I don't know if I have a move. I don't know why I'm even here, if *I* can be honest with *you*. I can't help anybody. I'm the wrong guy!" I am shouting crazy at the crow now. Then I turn to the crowd of wailing dogs who haven't done anything to me or to anybody else but just want to get out of a really bad situation. "I don't know what to do for you!" I shout. "I'm sorry. I'm really sorry."

The handlers of the dogs shift back and forth, murmur to one another. The dogs look like someone has just physically siphoned off half their blood. Several of them just lie down right there, sinking to the turf lifelessly.

How can this be? How can I . . . I, me, *I, I, I* have the ability to pick these guys up or drop them down just like that? Especially when I don't have any power to do anything about it?

"I'm sorry, guys," I call out again as I run across that track, trying to run as fast as any of them could run it. But I know I just look stupid. Everyone from the sock rabbit on back to the last-place dog to probably the handlers could run laps around me. The only advantage I have over the rabbit — and the dogs — is that I can leave the track when I want to.

But it's a whopping great advantage.

Even as I'm leaving, I hear them moaning, and the sound is in my head heating it up, like my brain is in an oven.

"Yeah, well, it's even worse for them," says the rat in the vest as I race past him for the exit. "It's like that for them all the time."

"You can't make me," I tell Hugo once I'm home. When I got back, he looked at me with such expectant eyes. But what was he thinking? How could I be anything but a disappointment?

"Then make yourself," he replies.

"No. You can't make me, and I can't make me. Hugo, I'm sorry, but how many animals do you really think I can save? I can barely save myself. Hire somebody else. Get all the animals to march on the White House. I have studying to do and I need a bath."

Hugo is giving me the soulful and scathing stare, but I'm not having it. I go into my bathroom and ask it to get my bath running. The bathroom knows exactly what temperature I like.

But I stop before I can get a word out. My bathtub is . . . occupied.

"Why are there fish in my bathtub, Hugo?" I ask. "Who put fish in my bathtub?"

Yes, there are fish in my bathtub. Those fat bubble-eye orange-and-black Japanese goldfish. I have never met these fish before. This is my private bathroom, which nobody uses but me, so there is no reason unexplained bubble-eyed fish should be in my tub.

"Hugo?" I call.

He comes ambling in and stands next to me looking into the tub.

"You've got some fish," he says.

"I know I do. *Where did they come from?*"

"My guess is Japan."

"I am not in the mood, Hugo. I want these fish out of here. I need my bath. I need my warm bath right now."

Warm baths are kind of my salvation. I really like warm baths, and in almost all instances when life or whatever else is overwhelming me, I retreat to the security of my enveloping warm bath.

Without fish.

"Hey," Hugo says, "they're only animals, right? If they are inconveniencing you, flush 'em."

"Flush 'em?"

"Yeah, flush 'em."

The stress and the lack of a warm bath are really getting to me now. I can sense the bathrooom's about to ask me what's wrong. And the last thing I want is my bathroom to talk to Room, which will then talk to my parents.

"Maybe I *will* flush them," I say.

"Maybe you should."

"Don't tempt me, dog."

"I'm tempting you, kid."

Arrgghh. Everybody knows I am not flushing anybody.

I groan and slump to the floor with my back to the bath, which should now contain me and warm water and not fish.

Hugo sidles up to me, sits down, and lets his warm little body press against my side.

"Those dogs were so sad, Hugo. I can still see their faces, hear their moaning. . . . I need a bath."

"There is no other guy, Zane. You are our guy, and you know it. You're just going to have to be a little brave about it."

"I hate being brave. Being brave scares me."

Beep. In the bedroom I hear Gizzard™ calling. It's a text-beep. I have yet to hear my father's voice through the noodle. He likes texts. He likes the precise thought that goes into them, and the control, like baking a cake from scratch rather than from a box. You know, the personal touch.

"Keep an eye on the fish while I'm gone," I say to Hugo.

"Of course. I love fish."

My little Gizzard™ screen is already covered in electric green type by the time I pick it up. *Why is your bathwater so cold?* my father wants to know. *Is everything all right?*

Of course, everything is all right. I check my PhysioMonitor just to be sure. Vital signs look pretty vital.

Slow news day, Father? I type with my thumbs.

Up on the big screen, my Newsmama pops up, looking nicely buffed for a holiday Monday morning. She is doing a puff piece on Christopher Columbus for Columbus Day. She's standing in front of a restaurant by the harbor. The wind is blowing, but her hair is not. I turn the sound down when she starts talking about pizza.

Hey, does a father need a slow news day to express concern for his child's well-being?

Hugo strolls into the room.

"Does my father need a slow news day to express concern for his child's well-being?" I ask him.

"Yes," Hugo says.

I flip the telescreen to a sports feed, and the scene changes from the lovely waterfront to the less lovely dog track. I do believe I see some faces I know. I turn up the volume.

"And I have to tell you, people, I've seen them in action, and these guys just live to run," the sportscaster says. "I have never seen anything like these fine little athletes, and if you want to see them, get yourselves down to the track today for the annual Columbus Day race. Half-price admission for everyone who shows up in one of those baseball hats with the floppy dog ears."

"Which they will promptly cut off of you," Hugo snarls. "They don't let any of their own dogs have floppy ears."

As if on cue, behind the sportscaster, a whole pack of the dogs begin straining toward the camera, barking and fussing like they just cannot wait for the party.

In my ear, though, loud and clear, I hear it all different.

"What about it, Zane? What about us?"

I grab both of my ears and squeeze them hard, trying to keep out any more sound, trying to wring out the awful words that already got in.

What about it, Zane? are my father's words typed on the screen in my hands. I have no idea what he has been going on about the last few minutes. *What about it? Think it's a good idea? I think it could be great.*

Sure, Dad, I type just to make it all stop. *Sounds great.*

I sign off and head for the bath. The only thing in my way is Hugo. Hugo, and the telescreen's remote control, which he has under his paw. He is spread out flat on the floor looking up at the telescreens.

"What about it, Zane?" Hugo asks, repeating, I guess, today's secret phrase. Did somebody change my name without telling me? Whataboutitzane? Whataboutitzane?

"What about it, Hugo?" I snap. "Great, cool, I'm impressed. You can work the remote control without any articulated digits. Bravo."

He is repeating the sportscast of the racetrack. He is

backing up over the drawn faces of the dogs, backing up over their cries, *What about it, Zane? What about us? What about it, Zane? What about us?* Back and forth and back and forth like a truck running over a body and returning repeatedly until the guy is good and brutalized.

"What about it, yourself," I say, going up and snatching the controller from him. I start flipping channels and screens all over the wall, all over the world, visiting life on Earth in all its demented glory.

"What about *this*," I say as we lock on a scene of Biblical scale, whole mountainsides of California sliding into the Pacific ocean. "You gonna fix this, Hugo?" I flip to another scene of hundreds of people, lots of kids, in raggedy heavy clothes all milling around in a big cage that looks a lot like the dog track. "You gonna solve the refugee problem while I'm out making the world a safer place for stuffed rabbits?" I flip again and find highlights of the Boston Bruins losing 8–2 to the Montreal Canadiens. A graphic says it's the sixteenth consecutive time the Canadiens have beaten the Bruins. "And the Canadiens aren't even that good!" I shout at my dog. "Who can do anything about that?"

It is possible I am losing perspective toward the end there, but Hugo sees my point.

He lies there flat on the floor and mute. Just like a good dog should. I step right over him and head for the comfort of my bath.

I drop to my knees beside the tub and dip my fingers in the water. Perfect. My bath is never wrong. I close my eyes for a second.

And he's right on my heels, literally, standing on my heels. The hairy little guiltwad.

"The difference is, those are things neither one of us can do a lot about. The difference is, if you have a special ability, a gift, a power, you should probably do something special with it."

I can just vaguely recall a time when I thought a talking dog was a good idea.

"What are you going to be, Zane — just one more fancy machine, sitting in your room full of fancy machines?"

My head weighs a thousand pounds. As his words settle inside it, I can feel the heaviness behind my eyes, filling me up and pulling me down, until . . .

Plunk, my head is down, and submerged, in the water. It is now warm and perfect and quiet and the best place I have ever been, fish or no fish. I hold my head there, and it is no effort at all.

Hugo has followed me into my waterworld. At least, his voice has. He comes clear through the noodle, and doesn't sound underwater blubby at all.

"If you don't want to be a machine, Zane, I guess you have to be a man."

My head now weighs one thousand and fifty pounds, because it's waterlogged. But it is still no effort to yank myself up out of the bath and onto my feet. My large hair is saturated, and pouring rain down on the little dog who looks straight up at me now. "From now on," I say, "I'm going to *enjoy* burning ticks out of you."

I leave my precious bath that is not to be, and I walk over Hugo on the way out. "I knew right along you wouldn't let us down," he says.

I spin and point at him in a firm authoritative way intended to create the illusion I have some kind of power. "Okay, I'm going," I say, "but you'd *better* have a bath waiting for me when I get back because I am going to need it."

"I can't talk to the bathroom yet — it won't understand me."

"Then do it the retro way and run the taps."

"Can't do that, either. No thumbs, remember?"

"Yeah, well I have no courage, either, but here I go. I guess we'll both have to evolve pretty quickly, huh?"

He snarffle-laughs at me. But it's okay, it's the good laugh.

"You're *Our Friend*," he says proudly.

WHATABOUTITZANE?

The track seems almost like a place transformed from what I visited earlier. It's amazing what real people and a flurry of activity can do to make a place seem lifelike.

There are hundreds and hundreds of people buzzing around in the streets and parking lot outside the track. The sounds of lots more are coming from the inside. The sun is shining, music is playing, and there is a general air of carnival about the place.

"You can't come in here," the gate attendant says. It is an older woman with lemon-yellow hair and half the usual number of teeth, all on the bottom.

"Why not?" I ask, money plainly visible in my anxious fist.

"No unaccompanied minors," she says, pointing behind her to one of several metal signs hanging off the chain link. She's actually pointing to a sign that says NO LOITERING, but debating it probably won't help.

"But I was just here. Jo-Jo gave me a tour. Just ask him."

She doesn't say a word, just points back to the sign.

Since there doesn't appear to be any reason left for politeness, I tell her, "That sign doesn't say what you say it says," I say.

Without looking, she points to another sign, threatening to have me towed at my own expense.

"Is there a problem here?" I know the voice behind me right away and it gives me a chill.

"No probs, Doc," the lady says to Dr. Gristle. "Just an underager trying to get in."

"Well," he says, laying a hand on my shoulder, "that's fine. Zane's here with me."

And now I'm stuck with him, too.

The woman scowls at me. "Why didn't you tell me you was with the doc?"

"I got confused," I say, "with all the signs and everything. You know how it is."

"I sure do, tiger," she says, and makes that clicky cheek noise like people do to horses. It makes my hair stand on end.

But she has waved us on through, and I am now inside the exciting racing scene with my new nemesis, Dr. Gristle.

"Hi," I say as he gives my neck a pinchy squeeze.

"Have you given any more thought to bringing back

my animals that you stole? They are really very special to me."

"I never stole any animals, Dr. Gristle. I suppose maybe, when I was exercising them, a few might have slipped away. I forgot, you see, that some of them were climbers. I was only trying to help." I don't specify *who* I was trying to help.

"I need them back, Zane. They are important to me. I can tell you love animals as much as I do, and so you will appreciate that my work with animals is very important. To animal kind and humans alike. My work is very, very important. It could make the whole world a better place for everybody. Wouldn't you like to be part of something like that, Zane?"

He is marching me across the grounds toward the animal enclosures like he is guiding me to my cell.

"You're hurting my neck, Dr. —"

"Sure you would. Of course you would. This work is very important, and you could be very important, too. Everyone would like to be very important, and famous, right?"

"To tell you the truth, famous isn't something I think about a lot. Everybody seems to know my parents, and from what I can tell it doesn't make life any easier than it otherwise would be. In fact, I might like it better if —"

I thought that mentioning my parents might get him to loosen his grip. But no. It gets even tighter.

"Your parents are great," he says. "They're two of the

greatest people I have ever known. I have a lot of respect for them and what they do, and that is one reason, out of respect for them as well as your obvious and passionate love of animals, that I have not turned you over to the investigators. Believe me, they have ways of making kids talk. And of making them feel very, *very* uncomfortable. Speaking of which, how did you get those bats to attack me in the woods there? That was great stuff. What's your secret?"

I'd shake my head, but at this point I can barely move it.

"I don't have any secret, Dr. Gristle."

"Of course you do. Everyone has secrets, Zane."

I almost wish he wouldn't smile. We are walking and talking and about to enter the tunnel under the stands where the dogs live, and he is still squeezing my neck and he is smiling like he's on a game show. It's a powerful megawatt smile and it is not reassuring at all.

"I didn't make the bats get you, Dr. Gristle."

"Right," he says, letting go of me as we go inside, where other people can see us. "Hello, hello, hello," the doctor says to the dog handlers who are hanging out with the dogs, apparently expecting us. "Let's get started, so these fine athletes can get out there and give these good people the show they deserve, eh?"

Nobody answers him. In fact, the whole thing feels a little bit tense, as if something serious were at stake before the dogs even leave the locker room.

"Okay, okay, okay," Dr. Gristle says as he goes up and down the lineup for inspection. He gives each dog a groping, ribs, legs, hips, everywhere. He looks in the ears. "See this, Zane," he says, and I look close inside the ear. There is a number tattooed in there. "This identifies each dog and his owners, just so we know who is who in case anything funny is going on. No tattoo, no racing."

"What kind of funny?" I ask.

"Not funny at all," he says. "Do you see me laughing?"

"Sorry," I say.

"No need to be sorry. You're just learning."

He's acting like I'm his prize pupil. But it's really his way of not letting me out of his sight. I don't know how I can help the dogs if I can't get free of Dr. Gristle first.

"This dog's not running," he says to a handler.

"Why not?" the handler asks.

"Because he's from the K-10 Club, and they've been banned for six months for dog doping. Get him out of here."

Dog and handler slink away, tails between legs. Dr. Gristle turns to me, teeth gritted. His eyes are red, as if he's the one who's been doped.

"I can't *stand* that," the doctor says, and from his look I have to believe him. "I cannot stand the thought of somebody putting performance-enhancing drugs into such beautiful, sensitive, highly tuned creatures. It makes me crazy."

Well, something certainly does.

But he is sincere. He is tearing up as he tells me this, and when he turns back around to examine the next hopeful racer, it is with intensity and warmth that I don't think could be fake.

"And how are you today, love?" Dr. Gristle says right into the snout of a trembling gray skinnybones. "You've heard of horse whisperers," he says to me. "I am a dog whisperer. I speak to them just so, and they speak back to me, in their own way."

I watch with fascination as he leans even closer and starts talking softly right into the nostrils of the lucky dog.

"Will somebody get this goon out of my nose, please?" the dog says. But I'm the only one who can understand it.

"She's feeling very serene," he says. "She's going to race well tonight."

"He smells like gasoline and wormer pills. I think I'm going to be sick."

For the most part, the inspection goes okay, and the dogs are given the go-ahead to head out onto the track. Some of them, to my eye, look like they would not make one full circuit at an easy trot, they look so tired and stringy, but there's nothing I can do about it. Not yet, anyway. I need a plan. Maybe it was foolish to rush back here (thanks, Coach Hugo, getting me all fired up and shoving me in the game without a helmet), but I'd feel even more foolish if I was staying away.

Last up is the stud, the star attraction, SureShot. Jo-Jo himself is handling him.

It doesn't take long for Dr. Gristle to have an opinion.

"This dog is not running," he says immediately.

"'Course he's runnin'," Jo-Jo says. "It's what he does."

The doctor's disrespect for the likes of Jo-Jo is hard to miss. "Well, it's not what he does today."

"Why not?"

"You know why not."

"There's a lot of money bet on that dog, Doc. You don't want to spoil everybody's day, do you?"

"I don't mind," Dr. Gristle says.

It's tense. Jo-Jo has filled the whole area with his presence. He's not threatening the doctor, exactly, but he is a threatening figure just the same.

The doctor, though, despite his long, wiry, pale appearance, despite his boyish blond head way up there on that tall lightweight structure, is having none of it. He is leaning right back in Jo-Jo's direction.

"I won't tolerate dogs on steroids," Dr. Gristle says. "Once my test is confirmed, the kennel owner is suspended, and if this keeps up on your track, you'll be out of business as well."

Funky little code of ethics he's got there. The man who likes to wire dogs "for their own good," clearly doesn't like other ways of controlling them. It's a little inconsistent, to say the least, but he doesn't seem to notice. I keep quiet.

"Come on, Zane," he says. "We need to get out on the track and observe the racing."

We head back out into the sporting arena. Just before we exit, I hear Jo-Jo call to me, "Don't forget to get me on your parents' shows, now."

He's still expecting a full media parade.

"Sure thing," I say.

Out on the track, things are heating up. The dogs' muzzles and racing colors make them look like demented cybodogs as they get lined up for the start. The announcer is whipping everything up, making the coming race sound like a cross between the Academy Awards and a demolition derby. The crowd, filling about half the stadium, does more whooping than cheering, but they are apparently happy to be here.

I seem to be the only human around who senses something deeply wrong.

What now, Hugo? I ask.

Suddenly, a booming P.A. voice shouts, "And, there goes Swifty!"

Swifty is the rabbit made of old socks and wire.

Who would chase this thing? What must their lives be like, if they think of this as a fun or important thing to do?

"It's amazing what you'll do when you don't have a choice," observes the rat sitting on my shoe.

We are in special box seats, in the first row of the stands. Without my noticing, the rat has settled into his even more special seat. Normally, this would have me screaming, kicking, and/or fleeing, but there is a reassuring air about this particular vermin. Maybe it's the vest.

"Listen to Rattus," he says.

"Are you listening to me?" Dr. Gristle asks.

"I am," I say to both of them.

"Number sixteen," Gristle says. "Bluetooth. He's going to win."

"How do you know that?"

"Oh, he knows," Rattus tells me. "That dog's a freak."

"Oh, I know," Gristle replies mysteriously. "That dog's special."

As he says that, it's like a bell has rung, and he has to go into action. The dogs have reached the halfway point in the race. And while it doesn't look like Swifty is in any immediate danger, several of his canine admirers are awfully close, including number sixteen.

"Who's a special boy?" Dr. Gristle says softly into the heel of his thumb. "Who's a champion? Fast. Fast. Rabbit. Yours. Yours. Fast. Speed."

I look, with amazement and chill, as the doctor gives his hand a pep talk. Then I look back out to the track where Bluetooth is starting to put some distance between himself and the rest of the field, getting closer and closer to ol' Swifty.

"See?" Rattus says. "Freak."

"Are you doing that, Dr. Gristle?" I ask.

"Don't be absurd, Zane. He is doing it himself. He's a champion." His voice drops as he speaks to the thumb again. "You are a champion. And a very pretty boy."

I look to the rat for sanity.

"He does stuff, with the dogs. Some of them. He . . . manipulates. But they always test clean. The ones he works with run like horses. But they wind up mad as Dalmatians."

The crowd is in full roar now, as if this were a normal sporting event, except that this crowd has onion-stink breath when it joins forces. Bluetooth is running away with it and is only inches from the rag-fluffy tail sock of brave Swifty. The next closest dog as they cross the line is about five yards back, which is about five yards ahead of the next one. The last-place dog, the gray skinnybones Dr. Gristle referred to as "serene," is so far behind she may end up being in the next race. Any more serene and the doc is going to need his defibrillator paddles.

We practically beat her to the finish line as we bound down out of the stands toward the competitors. Dr. Gristle's got a gleam in his eye, and I feel I have to follow him to find out what's going on.

"Watch it," Rattus says when I nearly punt him out of the stadium.

"Sorry," I say.

Dr. Gristle is clearly very anxious to see Bluetooth. Bluetooth, I notice, looks a little less keen to see the doctor.

"That was very impressive," Gristle says, speaking weirdly and softly again as he looks deeply into the dog's eyes. "You're the boy. You're the king. You're the boy king."

I swear, the other dogs look embarrassed for him.

"Does he own this dog?" I ask Rattus on the sly. I am talking low, out of the side of my mouth, trying to be cool and inconspicuous so as not to attract unwanted attention. Then I notice that everybody at the racetrack looks like that.

"Nobody owns a dog," Rattus says angrily. "Get that right, first. Nobody owns a dog, or a rat, or a fish —"

"Or a cat, or a frog. I understand now. Sorry."

"Who said anything about cats? Cats are jerks. You can own a million cats if you want to."

Now is *not* the time for me to be arguing cats' rights with a rat. "Anyway," I murmur, "you know what I mean. Is this dog, like, his, in that way?"

"No, he's just Doc's experiment. This one kennel went for it . . . and the bad news is, it's working. Now, who knows where it goes?"

An experiment? I want to ask more, but people are starting to look at me and my murmurs. I just have to pay closer attention. Bluetooth might be a key to what's going on around here . . . and what I'm supposed to stop.

While Dr. Gristle is flattering and humiliating the winner, the loser is having a quieter time of it. Gray skinny-bones is being practically dragged across the infield of the track by somebody with a wicked scowl on his face. She is trying with all her might not to follow, but her might is probably not good enough at the best of times, and right now she's got all the fight of a kite.

"No-no-no-no-no," she's saying. But for once I don't think she's saying it to me.

"Wouldn't want to be her," Rattus says sadly.

"Would you want to be *him*?" I ask, gesturing toward the winner with a veterinarian up his nose.

The dogs from the first race are all just about off the track now as the runners for the second go are led on. Dr. Gristle heads back toward his perch to watch the action again. He is very excited, animated. He looks the same way the dogs do as they ready for the race, running a little zigzag pattern toward his destination, breathing hard.

I follow at a safe distance. But not safe enough.

"Did you see that, Zane?" he says. He has doubled back to collect me and is now pulling me along by the hand. He has nobody else to tell, and he has to tell *somebody*. It appears to make no difference to him — nor to anybody in the whole place, for that matter — that we have a chubby well-dressed rat trotting along beside us. "He was beautiful. We did it. We actually did it!"

"Can I ask what we did, Dr. Gristle?"

"We chipped in!" he says, grabbing me by both shoulders and shaking me in a scarily friendly way.

He keeps shaking, like I'm supposed to join in or

something. The best I can do for him is to stare vacantly. And be shaken, of course.

"Chipped to win!" he clarifies, sort of. "That dog, Bluetooth, was carrying a new Gristle chip in him when he blew the whole field away just then. He was a good dog before, but he is a superdog now."

"Is that allowed?"

"Yes! Yes! All natural, perfectly legal. This is what is so wondrous about all this, my boy. We — meaning I — have the power to alter things, to improve animals dramatically with the strategic implementation of the right chip, combined with the input of an intuitive handler — like myself. The applications are unlimited. All kinds of creatures can be better better better, improved, reimagined to greater and greater heights, and we will not have to resort to the horrors I have seen with steroids and amphetamines and other chemical atrocities. Life for animals and for me and for everybody can change from this point onward and there is no downside. All that money that the government's poured into the lab — well, now they'll see results!"

He is, by the way, still shaking me by the shoulders. He is so fired up there is no doubt in my mind he could win the upcoming race, which is about to start.

"You, my boy, have gotten in on the early stages of one of the most dramatic developments in the history of humankind."

It's like he's completely forgotten that I freed his

animals. This one animal is the only one that matters to him right now.

"Sounds pretty big, Doctor," I say, trying to keep him talking, so I can learn as much as I can. I figure that's what Hugo would want me to do.

"*Big?* Zane, did you not hear me? It will be far bigger than big. It's going to be so big it's going to make big look . . . small! We can make every animal there is better and I will be famous, and that is about as big as a thing gets, don't you think?"

If I were a braver person, I would suggest he dig around in his bag and get out a rabies shot for himself. I'm not a braver person, though.

"Now that you put it that way, I see what you mean. Can I go and check on the dogs instead of watching this second race?"

"What?" He looks around, goes wide-eyed as if he's surprised to find that there are still dogs here running circles around his universe. "Oh. Yes, I suppose so. I need to have a look at a feisty fellow in this second running. You go on. I'll see you on the infield after this one. Because the two of us still have some business to transact."

"Right," I say, running straight off, with my trusty rat in tow.

We make it halfway across the track when the announcer booms out, "And there goes Swifty!"

Uh-oh.

You know that thing, deer and headlights? That's me in the middle of the dog track, comin' atcha live. You wouldn't think skinny weightwatcher racing dogs with muzzles would be the most intimidating beasts on Earth, but holy moly. There are thirteen or fourteen of them, and they all have twelve legs and their determined carnivorous faces look like they are going to explode like whiskered rockets out of their face masks. I'm thinking NFL linemen only with much bigger teeth as they come shooting right at me.

I'm frozen. Rattus, on the other hand, has scampered away like the faithless rat he is.

Swifty passes by on the rail, lifeless and blistering as a bullet train.

"Off the track, numbskull," Rattus spits.

He snaps me to life just in time to nose-dive off the track and into the infield.

The sound, as I lie there on the grass with the dogs pounding by, is like hearing a hundred drummers pounding away at the head of a parade. I look up to watch them lean into the turn and am stunned again at the intensity, at the absurd perfection of the dogs' running and their mad determination to get there, wherever *there* is.

I get up, and bolt across the middle of the oval and cross the far side of the track before the runners can get there. I am over and into the enclosure when I hear the roar for whatever great champion has managed it this time.

"Over here," Rattus is calling me. It is an extremely good thing that I have him as a guide to this unseemly underworld, because there is no way I could negotiate the dark corridors of this sporting underbelly on my own. I can't even see where he's at, but I follow the sound of his voice. It smells worse than when I visited earlier, probably because of the added pungence of competition. Like a post-game locker room, only doggified. There is wild panting everywhere, too, and the slapping lapping sound of creatures who are drinking water to save their lives.

"Here," Rattus says.

This, I guess, is the winner's circle. It is a darkened cage down the end of a darkened corridor. Inside it, the great champion Bluetooth is pacing back and forth and back and forth, breathing in gasps. He stops to drink water, which he is clearly desperate to do, but then violently pulls his face up out of the bowl again because he has to keep pacing.

I can hear his heartbeat. And his nonstop talk to himself.

"Can't run that fast, can't. Can't run that fast. Too fast. Too fast. Never run, never run. Too fast. Can't."

He stops for more water, drinks for two seconds, and goes back to pacing and jabbering.

And crying. He is crying desperately. I feel uncomfortable, lost and scared at the same time as I watch this magnificent beast in his cage, the little bits of light shooting from I don't know where but playing on Bluetooth's crazy muscles as he weeps like a pup. He seems more lost than I do as he walks and cries and drinks and jabbers in his little cage when it's absolutely *not* what he is meant to be doing.

"Notsofast," he goes on. "Notsofast. NoNoRabbitRabbit-Rabbit."

"What is wrong with him?" I demand, actually grabbing Rattus by what are sort of his little lapels. As if he were the source of Bluetooth's distress, and I were somehow the solution.

"I think he's running too fast."

"But that's what he's supposed to do. There's no such thing as too fast in his world."

Suddenly, Bluetooth starts pacing faster and faster around his cage, kind of nutty-like.

"See," I say, "he's itching to go again."

Which I know is not true. He's not in control here. It's painful to watch and I want it to stop.

"Slow down, boy," I say, pressing up close to his cage. "Easy now. Look, can't you be more like her?"

I refer, of course, to the cage across the hall, which holds the unfortunate gray skinnybones. She is flat out on her side, adhered to the floor like she's been nailed down.

I don't know if he's actually listening to me or what, but Bluetooth abruptly sits down awkwardly. It's a very unnatural-looking thing, with his back legs splayed wide and his front legs propped like they're battling to keep him from toppling onto his face.

A handler ambles down the corridor and pays us no mind whatsoever. Business as usual goes on.

"Good," he says to the lifeless skinnybones. "That's right, just do what you do best, ya stiff. Because you won't be doin' it around here anymore." He gives her cage a sharp kick before going on to cheer up some other lucky loser. Skinnybones has no response.

This is not good.

"What does he mean?" I ask Rattus. "What's going to happen now?"

"Oh, don't worry," he says, "they'll take care of her."

"Really?" I say, believing a little because I want to believe a lot.

"Absolutely. First they'll chop off her ears so she can't be identified by her tattoos, then they'll dump her in the woods someplace."

Right now, I hear Skinnybones crying. Lying still flat as a rug, but sobbing.

"That's your idea of taking care of her?"

"Well, she won't have to race anymore. She really hates racing more than she likes being alive. Most of them do. So, in that way she'll be better off."

I have to do something.

Bluetooth is back to pacing. It's like it is killing him to keep pacing, but he is possessed to keep pacing. And I swear

I do hear his heart beating from here. I hear her sobbing and his beating like it's all being piped over the loudspeakers.

"This is the saddest place on Earth," I say.

"Take it from a rat, kid — there are lots of saddest places on Earth. That's where you usually find us. And yeah, this is one of 'em. Life happens, I guess, and you just gotta let it."

"No," I say, stepping right over and opening up Bluetooth's cage, "you don't gotta."

Ever seen a rat smile? It is one of life's really unsettling sights, even when it's a good thing.

"I was hoping you'd say that," Rattus says.

I kneel down in front of the nerve-wracked dog, and I stroke his face, his soft satiny head. I scratch his chest to calm him down.

"If you talk into my nose right now," Bluetooth says, "I cannot be held responsible for my actions."

"I won't," I promise. "But I'm thinking about getting you out of this place. What say?"

He knocks me flat over in his rush for the door.

I walk straight across and open the other cage. Skinnybones barely raises her head. I pick her up and drape her over my shoulders like a fur stole. A bone stole, more like.

One dog by my side, another on my back, I make my way through the windy, dank corridor toward the exit. One of the last cages we pass contains the former favorite and future jailbird, SureShot. He starts throwing himself against his cage door. *Bang, bang.* They should have let him run, just to get his ya-yas out. *Bang*, he hits it again and the door flies open.

As I exit the enclosure, we are a team, a parade, an uprising. I grab a couple of leashes off the hooks at the door, and bring my followers somewhat under my control.

"What's going on?" I ask Rattus. I figured they'd put up more of a fight.

"I guess you got magnetism."

"I don't want magnetism."

"And I don't want a big fat butt, but whatcha gonna do?"

I look back over my shoulder to see Rattus standing in the doorway watching us go, seeing us off like we all just had a nice pleasant dinner at his house.

"You're not coming?" I ask.

"Hey, I'm a rat. I don't need nobody's help to come and go as I please. I got work here. I'll see you again. Plus, you're going to need my help."

He's referring to Jo-Jo, who is standing now in that same doorway. Glowering in our direction, he points a big sausage finger my way and bellows, in choppy nasty phrases, "Don't you . . . go nowhere . . . with my beasts."

I am frozen. I'm far enough away and young and slim enough that outlegging the man would not seem to be a problem, but he is menacing enough to knock sense cleanly out of the equation.

Fortunately, there is the magnificent Rattus. He makes a little salute wave like skydivers do, then shoots himself right at the baggy steel-blue, oily-stainy pant leg of the most unsanitary man I have ever seen.

Jo-Jo tries to jump with such force, his feet almost leave the ground.

Rattus is right back down again. "Oh, mercy," he says, holding one little hand over his vested chest and panting sickly. "I've got family stretching all the way back to the Black Death, but there is *nothing* in my history to compare to the horrors up there." He points up at the pants.

I am overcome by his bravery. I give him a thumbs-up and break away, as he holds his breath and goes once more into the breach.

Jo-Jo is screaming, and throwing his bulky self right down on the ground as we make our getaway.

I salute to the memory of one brave rat, then notice again just what I've got going here. Two highly agitated and demented-looking dogs bouncing on powerful pistons behind me, and one flacid and surprisingly weighty Skinnybones on top of me. I turn and see the ticket lady sitting on an upturned trash barrel by the parking lot gate.

"Be cool," I say to the dogs.

"Rabbit," Bluetooth says. "Rabbitrabbit."

We make it to the gate.

"What are you up to, Junior?" the yellow hair lady asks me through a cloud of smoke all around her head. I see no evidence of a cigarette, but whatever.

"I'm . . . Doc wants these two to get some wind-down exercise," I say. "They are still pretty edgy from the race."

The dogs do their part, knowingly or not. They strain at the leashes, walk excitedly around me, tie my legs up, bump into one another, growl.

"And what about that one?" the lady asks.

"Oh," I say, just now remembering. "Ah, he wants me to get some exercise, too. This is my workout, carrying the dog. On the way back, we switch. This one walks and one of them gets the royal treatment."

"You are not carrying me! I can run!" Bluetooth says.

"Well," she says, "if the doc says so . . ."

"He does." The bunch of us scurry out the gate, down the street, around the corner as fast as our legs can carry us.

And our legs, it turns out, can carry us quite fast. Even with Skinnybones aboard, I've got the two mad dogs for freedom yanking me along and it's like a chariot race. My feet rarely touch pavement as we make it all the way back to the WildWood. It takes us a while, but it doesn't feel that way.

It's almost like I don't have to lead them. Bluetooth ticks every turn right along with my mind. Like he knows what I want him to do without me having to say it.

Strange.

I will never get away with this. I don't know what I was thinking, bringing three racing dogs to the WildWood. I mean, what now?

It's not as if my heroic efforts are universally appreciated even in the animal realm.

"Why don't you just leave everybody alone?" Goth Sloth wants to know. "Why do you keep coming here? You don't belong. You don't understand us at all. What's the point? What's the point of anything? What are those dogs doing here? I'm not sharing. Why does everything happen to me? I'm hungry. I'm tired. What are you looking at? Stay out of my stuff. None of your business. You'll be sorry when I'm dead. The whole world is against me."

Go, world.

I wouldn't say GS is representative of animal opinion, but right now I find myself with my head in my hands, walking kind of aimlessly around the woods with a sinking feeling that I am very much on my own.

Then I hear someone calling my name . . . and I wish I *was* alone.

"Zane! I know you're in here."

It's Dr. Gristle. He's here in the woods. I can't get away from him.

"Go away!" I call out, heading for the water. "I'm not here."

"Neither am I," he answers. "And neither are all the missing animals — including those greyhounds you just stole. I know they are here, Zane, even if I can't see them. I know, and you know I know."

I know.

"I saw you leave the track," he continues. "I followed you. I know what you're up to."

I hear him crunch-crunching after me, but he is falling off the pace as he trips and stumbles, curses, stumbles some more. He doesn't know this WildWood like the animals do. Even the ones who have not been here before know it as soon as they come into it, like it's their ancient natural home. Even if the tracking on the chips is still working, it'll take him a long time to catch them all.

"You cannot just go on stealing animals that don't belong to you, Zane," he calls out.

"Animals don't *belong* to anyone," I say. "And, yes, I can keep doing it. Because the animals aren't yours to have."

I have run the distance, to the WildWater's edge, where it is clear and light and not entirely reassuring. It's a bit dead-endy, unless you want to proceed into the water, which you don't if you want to live.

He has stopped, I can tell, in the middle of the woods. It's one of the things I admire about the WildWood — it defends itself against intruders. It has, no doubt, laid a scratching and a slapping and a whacking on Dr. Gristle, and he is already tiring of it. Good for you, Woods.

Still, he has enough breath to continue shouting at me. "What, like your dog? Like Hugo? He doesn't belong to you? He is free to come and go wherever and whenever he wants?"

"No, but that's not fair. Even I can't do that. When I leave my house's tracking system, my *room* even screams at me."

"That is love, Zane," Dr. Gristle calls out. "Don't you understand? That is concern, and concern is a sign of love. The fact that somebody thinks it is worthwhile to track and monitor and manage your every move is a beautiful and wonderful thing."

I am very glad there is a lot of hostile foliage between him and me right now. I wish there were more.

"Yeah?" I call back, angry, desperate, and confused, which is quite a soup to be in. "Who's watching you, then? I bet nobody."

There is a fizzy long silence in the cool leafy air between us.

"That was mean," he says.

Didn't see that coming. Just when you go thinking a guy's got no human feelings, there they are. Now I feel bad. I'm not like that. How did I get here? I never wanted to bother anybody all my life, as long as nobody wanted to bother me. Now here I am at the edge of the killer pond like Sherlock Holmes battling Professor Moriarty who happens in this case to be a deranged possibly genius veterinarian bent on animal world domination, and *I* am feeling bad about saying the wrong thing.

"Sorry about that," I call out.

"No need to shout," he says, emerging from the brush right in front of me. "All is forgiven."

He startles the guano out of me, and I backpedal four steps, right into the water.

It is no joke. It is no myth or urban legend. Even this little short way into the pond, I feel my legs all wrapped up, tangled in vines as thick and ropey as boa constrictors, and I am really stuck.

"Come out of there, you silly boy," Gristle says. "I'm not going to kill you. I'm just going to have you arrested and punished."

"I'm not so sure about that," I say. "And I'm not here by choice. I can't get out."

It's clear from Dr. Gristle's expression that he thinks this is just one more excuse from me, and he's getting very tired — almost violently tired — of excuses. "Of course you can," he says with a dismissive scowl. "Walk."

"I am trapped in vines, I'm telling you. If I could walk, I would. If you don't believe me, come on in."

"You must be joking. These are my one-of-a-kind television pants. Handmade in Hong Kong."

"Thanks, you're a sport. I can see your point. I'll just die now."

"Go ahead. Just *give me my animals back*. You have no idea — no idea whatsoever — who and what you're messing with."

I was concerned, remember, about hurting this guy's feelings.

"Are you going to help me?" I ask, all indignant with my hands on my hips and my pants drawing up water like a sponge.

Those words, that helpless plea, seem to have triggered something in the doctor's complicated and unsettling personality. His face goes rigid in a smile that looks like he is both truly happy and badly in need of a toilet.

"Maybe," he says.

"Maybe?"

"Maybe you need to help me first."

Rats. This cannot be happening. The vines are squeezing tighter and the water level feels like it's actually rising. Can ponds have tides? Oh, and it's very cold, like I fell asleep in the bath and woke up three months later in the same water.

Oh, my bath. Oh, if I could just be in my warm bath.

"How can I help you, Doctor?" I try to say this without sounding like a helpful shop assistant, but I think I fail. He claps his hands and rubs them together greedily.

"Just tell me your secret."

I am thinking that even under normal warm dry free-walking conditions that is one of the most unappetizing questions any kid could hear. Right now, it's appallingly insensitive.

"I don't have any secrets, I swear."

"Of course you do. Would you like to know mine?"

"I don't think I would, actually. Thanks all the same."

His patience is thinning again. Maybe this is one reason I have so few friends. There seems to be a time limit on how fun I am to be with.

"Come on, Zane. I'm not stupid. I know something is going on. You know about my work with the animals, how I can trace them, how I can read them, and the technology is quickly moving well beyond that. I have been running into *disturbances* with the program, and every time I do, things seem to lead back to you. Now, I will eventually work this thing out without your help, but that would put us in an adversarial position. We don't want to be in an adversarial position now, do we, Zane?"

If he were actually with me here in the water, holding me by the back of the neck and dunking my face in every few seconds, he could not be more menacing than he is right now.

"We don't want that, Doctor," I say.

"No, we don't. Now, I am going to let you in on a secret of mine, to show you my good faith, because I think you are special like me."

I'm about to tell him *I hope not* when he makes his big confession.

"I have a chip in me."

"I'd have guessed you were missing a chip or two, Doc," I tell him.

"Do you *like* it in there?" he asks. Seeing my freezing, scared reaction, he goes on. "Good. Now, this chip in me is going to change the world. To put it crudely, it is a sophisticated receiver, of information, from chipped animals. I am like a seer with animals now, able to suss out their needs and desires with great clarity. Even more important, it is a *transmitter*, for communicating my desires and demands into the individual animals. With this ability, humankind will be able to do all the little things — bossing their pets around, sending the dog out for cigarettes, that sort of thing. On the bigger stage, however, can you imagine the possibilities, of harnessing the power of an elephant, the speed of a cheetah, the senses of a bat . . . all for humankind's benefit? This will be huge. *Huge.* The world will be one wonderful, unified, human-animal partnership, and *I* will be master of it all."

Hmm. Maybe I don't want to come out of the water after all.

"I'm very happy for you," I say, shivering like my body's possessed by ice demons.

Gristle's face falls. "The problem is, it doesn't work."

I know I do myself absolutely no favors here, but I can't help it — I laugh out loud.

"See," he says, a mix of angry and sad, "that's what they will all do. They will all laugh at me if I do not sort the problem out. But when I do, they will all be laughing out of the other side of their faces. All of them."

Who are *they*? On second thought, I don't care.

"You know, Doctor, my parents will probably be pretty grateful if you save my life here."

"This isn't about you. And you're not even dying. Tell me your secret, Zane. You are somehow scrambling my pathway to the animals. It works sometimes, works a little, but then it doesn't. I know it's you."

My feet are sinking now, down into silty mucky stuff beneath the vines. What was uncomfortable and annoying before is sinking now to something that really is frightening.

"I need to get out of here."

"What's your secret, Zane?" He picks up a pretty big branch, something I could grab hold of while he pulled me back in. He raises it up . . . but then instead of extending it to me, starts lightly bopping me on the head and pulling it away again . . .

"This isn't funny."

Now it's Gristle's turn to laugh. "No, it isn't. This thing is bigger and more important than both of us, and must go forward no matter what it takes."

"Well, it doesn't take this."

"Maybe," he says viciously, "I don't need your secret. Maybe I just need you to *disappear*."

He is not this insane. I know this. He is just trying to scare me.

And he's doing an outstanding job.

"Somebody! Help!" I scream as loud as I can, knowing that never saved anybody from dying here before.

They weren't a Friend of the animals, however. I've sensed them watching, waiting for the doctor to maybe not be evil. Now it's time for them to hold up their part of the bargain.

I feel a tug. I feel a nudge. I feel, even, a sharp nibble. At first, I am freaked but quickly settle into the notion that anything is an improvement over the situation at hand.

Snap. A vine breaks. Snap, tug, grind — one by one the vines are being savaged by one of my underwater friends, my new best friend of any habitat.

Free. I have never known the kind of panic real physical confinement can bring. Being truly trapped is the worst. Being truly trapped by forces you can't see is worse than the worst.

So it is with an even greater joy that I find myself

bumped and lifted onto the back of my giant terrapin pal. I ride him like a very slow surfboard toward the land.

Dr. Gristle isn't laughing anymore. He can't see what is going on under the surface, but he can see I'm moving.

"Thank goodness, Zane! I would have helped, eventually," he says nervously. "You know that. In fact, I think, probably I did help . . . I made you fight, I got you inspired, so you would have the strength to . . . what *is* your secret, Zane?"

Now I am up out of the water, and it's like I'm riding the roof of a particularly bumpy small car. The terrapin is doing that freaky three-foot walk up the bank, foot-foot-face-foot, foot-foot-face-foot, and it is the good doctor's turn to be freaked and to backpedal and stumble away. Terrapin is charging. As much as a three-legged giant turtle can charge.

"I can't wait to tell my parents that you were going to let me die," I tell Dr. Gristle.

"You wouldn't."

"If you don't get out of here this second, I most definitely will."

"Fine," he says, dropping the branch he's holding and throwing up his hands. "But you've only made things worse for yourself. This was your chance to keep this between you and me, but now, it's going to have to escalate. I didn't want that. I don't necessarily want them to know *everything*, Zane.

You are more formidable than I thought. You've got something. You've got *my* something! But you're just a kid. You don't know the why and the how. We need to get the what and the why and the how together."

He's well on his way now, still talking, still walking.

"Whatwhyhow!" I call. "Whatwhyhow! There, I got them together, so don't bother."

"I'll have to bother, I'm afraid. But next time, I'm not coming alone. We want those animals back, and we will get those animals back. In the meantime, I want to know that secret of yours."

"My secret?" I say, standing triumphantly on the world's most awesome shiny turtle shell. "My secret is . . . I pick my nose."

EXODUS

It isn't easy to get a horned owl to trail a mad scientist, especially in the daytime. But if you ask nicely, it can be done.

"He's gone," Owl says, circling over me and the terrapin. "I gave him a full military escort, right out of the woods. And I dropped a packet on his shoulder as a parting gift."

"Nice touch," I say. "Thanks."

I am by now not lacking company. Starting with Mole, and then eventually — way eventually — Goth Sloth, the population of the WildWood has gathered around where I am sitting bankside next to Terrapin. A fox has draped himself over my back, watching over my shoulder and sharing his warmth. It has not been an uneventful time, and a staff meeting is pretty obviously required.

"Victory," proclaims a raccoon with his fisty claws in the air. A mad mash of animal voices cheers rises up in response. It's like a roaring earthquake of beastly noise and motion, but really it only makes me feel worse.

"Not really," I say when they have finally quieted down. Now you can hear a pine needle drop on the forest floor. "I mean, it was great to chase Gristle away, but not only is it just temporary, he's going to be coming back worse than before. He's coming with the forces. They want their experiments back, and they are built to get what they want. And we have to face facts — Gristle's right, I'm just a kid. I have what he wants, but he understands it and I don't. It is only a matter of time before he figures out every angle, but I am never going to understand the science of all this any better than I do right this minute."

Mole scurries over and climbs right up on my lap. He leans his warm furry self right into my abdomen. "It's not about science," he says. "It's about us."

I lay him gently back on the ground, slip off my fox cover, and stand up. "It's all about science," I say, "and that's the way we have to treat it. We have to be scientific about it, and not like a bunch of dumb animals and a dumb kid."

Bluetooth comes soaring past, like a regularly scheduled dog rocket. It's his second pass, and he disappears into the rough again.

"Can't somebody stop him?" I ask.

"The short answer is no," says Fox. "He's just got to run himself out. Don't worry about him — tell us what all the rest of us are supposed to do."

I look away, out beyond the WildWater, and point. "You guys have to clear out."

"All of us?" asks Fox.

"Every last one. As far as you can, out into the WildArea."

"That's just stupid," says Goth Sloth. On one level, it's kind of an honor to have him down here, closer to the ground than I have ever seen him. On another level, he's no more of a treat to talk to. "Nobody knows what's out there. And if they can track us here, they can probably track us down anywhere — so why bother going to all the trouble to, you know, *move* and stuff? This is my tree, in my woods, and nobody can make me do what I don't want to do. I just got it exactly the way I want it and nobody else is getting my place and probably this is just some kind of trick to get me to come down in the first place."

Between the volume and the speed of his disgruntle-ment, by the time GS finishes, I will have my space shuttle license and have removed most of the animals to the safety of Tralfamadore. So while he goes on, I talk to more ratio-nal beings.

"Mole, listen," I say. "This is big, it is military. They have resources, motivation, and very serious intentions."

The four o'clock Bluetooth whizzes by. I think he's actually *gaining* speed.

"The WildWood has been good to us," Mole says nervously.

I feel rotten for flushing them out, but there's no other way. "The WildWood will be a big bald patch on the face of the Earth, if that's what they need to do to get you guys back. If you leave it now, there is a chance you can come back to it someday."

The pin quiet is back as the animals take it all in. Up high in a tree, an owl hoots a long sad note.

"What about all the others still captive?" Fox wants to know. "And what about family? I don't know where my kits are . . . but I don't want to think I'm safe and they could be . . ."

"The family bit's not a problem here," says a gerbil peeking out of the base of a tree. "My mother ate two of my brothers. We're not really close."

"Right," I say. "Here's where we have to get tough. Nobody helps anybody by staying here. Spread out and survive, that's your job."

"And so, what's *your* job?" Goth Sloth demands.

"My job," I say, "is to make your job easier. And I think I have the beginning of the beginning of a plan."

By the time I slip into the house, night is coming down —
and that, I figure, is a good thing. I can feel the marching,
charging feet of Dr. Gristle and his Gristlies bearing down
on us even if nobody is exactly doing anything just yet.
Storm troopers are not likely to descend on a wood in darkness to try to collect a bunch of animals who are pretty
woodsy and very anxious to remain that way. Likely, we have
till morning before anything real happens.

If nothing else, I have time for a good, long overdue
bath. Among other things, it's the best place for thinking.

"What's my secret, Hugo?"

The bath temperature is just where I like it, because my
room knows exactly where I like it and when it starts to cool
off slightly my room turns on the coils to get it right back
where it belongs. My tub has claw feet, holding the whole
works up in the air above the heaters like I am some canni-
bal's dinner.

"It couldn't be the nose-picking thing, because every-body knows about that."

"See? I couldn't have a secret no matter how hard I tried. I would kill to have a real secret. When I fart, my room collects an air sample, processes it, and alters my menu accordingly. How could I have *any* secrets?"

"Everybody has secrets."

"That's what Dr. Gristle said."

Hugo has developed a kind of tick. At the mention of Dr. Gristle's name, he lets out a little involuntary (I think) growl.

"Grrr. He's right. He's wrong, very, very wrong, but he's right. Everybody's got secrets."

"Well, I don't."

Oh, and here's where he does it. Here's Hugo flexing his particular superpower.

That face. That wide-open, wide-eyed, head-thrusting, I-know-everything-there-is-to-know-in-the-universe-but-most-of-all-I-know-*you*-buster look. You know that look.

"I am your dog, remember," he says with the kind of generous laid-back cool you can afford when you are holding all of the cards. "I am your dog, and have held that job for a number of years now. Should we take a little trip down memory —"

"No, we shouldn't! I knew I should have put you out of the room. I *knew* it."

"Relax — I'm your best friend, right? There are no secrets between best friends."

"Well, that's very helpful, Friend, because I don't know what my own secret is, so could you tell me?"

"Your ear looks dirty. Wash your ears."

"Grrr," I say, and wash my left, Hugo-side ear. Then I go to wash the other one, and I'm stopped. The ear noodle, of course, is gumming up the works. I take it out and place it on the windowsill above the tub.

Silence. Absolute *silence*. I look all around the room, down at Hugo, up at the ceiling and while there are normal sounds in the air like the splash of the water and the passing of a car and whatever pointless nonsense is being broadcast on the various screens and speakers in my room, none of this is anything to me.

I stare hard at Hugo now and try to figure this one out.

It is so different. He is looking at me and he is a total blank. Is he doing it to me on purpose? How come he doesn't look like the sharp clued-in presence I have come to know and rely on since we've learned to talk?

"Say something to me," I say to him.

He blanks me. Not a twitch.

I am spooked. It's almost as if this Hugo is a different being from the other one, and I'm not saying he is trying to talk and I am just not hearing him, I am saying it feels to me like this Hugo is a lesser thing altogether, and I don't like it.

With only one clean ear, I quickly jam that noodle back into the waxy other one.

"Dog," I hear right away in that now-familiar Hugo voice. It's like he's been away forever.

"Say again?"

"Your secret. You're a dog, man. It's like having ears on your heart, so you can truly hear us. When the animals talk, you can receive it."

"I'm a dog."

"Congratulations on your promotion."

"Honestly, that's it? I can hear you and Gristle can't? Why can't he?"

"'Cause he's a jerk. Would you talk to a jerk if you didn't have to? All it takes is one good sniff and you can tell that guy's up to no good."

My bath is slightly cooling now, and I hear the heat come on underneath me. I start to get up, but I can't resist the warm water and settle back down.

"Tell me this — how come I'm hearing only some animals and not others?"

"Here is what I've been able to gather from comrades. Chips. It's those chips Dr. Nutso's been jamming into animals. The ones you have heard from are either pets, like me, whose families have agreed to the Gristle chip — thank you very much —"

"Sorry."

"Or it's the ex-pet community, pets whose families got them chipped before they escaped. Or, if it's not domestics, it's the experimentals, unfortunate saps who have been part of one Gristley experiment or another. They come from labs or zoos or his own private collection, but whoever they are, every chip tells a story. He's nuts with those chips, Zane, a very chippy guy. Some of these animal are escapees; some of them are still locked up. You have to save them all, by the way, and stay one step ahead of you-know-who the whole time. It's like he's everywhere."

"Don't I know it," I say. "He turns up everywhere I go. Then he seems to have some kind of source who's been telling him about me. It's all making me very uneasy."

So uneasy, in fact, I'm not even comforted by my nice bath anymore.

"Hugo, turn around. I'm getting out of the tub."

"Turn around?" he says, and does a hearty rendition of that snorting snarfling thing I now know is laughter. "I've seen this show a thousand times. I am your dog, you know.

"And I'm yours. Turn around."

"This is not canine behavior. Shame is for chumps."

"Fine," I say, "Then I will." I grab my towel and stand up with my back to my dog while I dry myself off.

"I know it is probably silly . . . from one dog to another, I have to tell you you really should lay off that fruit and vegetable nonsense. You need more protein, kid. Meat. Lots more meat."

I look over my shoulder to catch him looking the back of me up and down. He is shaking his big stupid head.

"I wonder what you would look like shaved totally bald?" This is me being tough.

"Pretty much exactly like you do right now," he says just before I grab him, and dunk him.

We are both clean and fluffy and refreshed as I step into my thick, post-bath bathrobe that makes me feel not only warm and soft, but thoughtful and smart. It's maroon, and has matching slippers. When I am in my maroon calming ensemble right out of my bath, the world slows down and starts making sense to me.

"I think I know what to do next, Hugo," I say quietly because the walls have ears. And eyes and antennae.

"Reporting for duty, sir."

"We need you to run away."

One of the few things Hugo does that you would call cute is when he pricks up his startled curiosity ears. "I was just starting to like it here," he says.

"I know, but as my second in command —"

"Don't kid yourself."

"Anyway, your service to the cause is twofold. I need

you to be scrammed out of here, and at the same time over-seeing the huge operation of the WildWood clearances."

Hugo pulls on his very serious face and his very serious voice. You'd have to know his face and voice to get it, and I get it.

"Will you pack me a snack?"

I pick him up and give him a good strong hug.

I don't care how much he kicks and scratches me.

I'm so revved up already, hours before I am supposed to get up. It's all I can do to fake sleep well enough to keep my whole room from zinging to life way before dawn.

But the sun is up, and it's time.

I sit up. Like I always do.

Then, on cue, my entire life sits up. Like it always does.

As the lights and the screens come on and the digital readout of my well-being or otherwise flashes and the Scent-o-Com sends me a message of pure maple-Belgian-waffle-and-Devon-cream delight and the ceiling wishes me good morning, I do the thing that every other ordinary boy does in the morning. I call my dog.

"Hugo!"

Hmm. No response. That is highly unusual.

"Hugo!"

Okay. Finally, it's time to get some use out of the mortal humiliation that was theater and mime class.

"No!" I shout, and hit the floor running, I flap and squawk and simper my way through every corner and cranny of the ZaneZone, looking for any Hugo-size lump that could plausibly be him, all the while playing shamelessly to the room and the speaker and every possible monitor I can trip. "Hugo, Hugo, Hugo . . ."

"Zane?" Room asks in a very calm voice, but I know better. Room can't deal with this kind of off-the-script . . . humanity. "Zane? Is there something the matter?"

I am jumping on my bed now, which is something I never do. I get so swept up in the power of my performance that I sprint from one end of the bed to the other and splat face-first into the wall, knocking myself flat on my back.

I am staring up into the ceiling speaker when That Voice rains down over me.

"Zane," Dad asks. "What the devil is the matter?"

"Hugo's gone," I say. "He's gone."

You'd have to look past my father's actual words to understand that he is truly concerned. But he is. "Easy, easy, Son. We'll get you another one, right away. What color was Hugo again?"

"He is not a *was*, he's alive. He's just not here. I have to get him back. He never does this. I'm really worried."

There is a silence. Things are not moving forward fast enough. I hold my breath long and hard and push my thumbs into my temples while my father discusses it with his staff or something.

An alarm goes off, like a tiny but serious fire station is springing to action under my bed.

It's me. I check my monitor wall. My blood pressure could be safely divided between two old smoker dudes. Heart rate — indicated by cute animal graphics — is just below hummingbird.

Those drama classes really did pay off.

"My goodness!" shouts the giant, gleaming pretty head of my mother high on the wall. "Zane, what is happening? Your charts are insane."

"Hugo's gone," I say. And because I know she is on a tight schedule and her maternal bull's-eye is fairly small, I go right for it. "And if I don't get him back right away I will die."

"Oh, no," she says. "Oh . . . dear . . ." She looks all around her in the studio. She checks her watch. She checks her look in the monitor.

My folks. They really are nice people. But if somebody hasn't typed it all out on a teleprompter in advance, they're kind of lost.

"We have to go to Dr. Gristle's," I say. "He has the tracking equipment. Then we can —"

"I'm dialing him right now," she says.

"No, don't . . . we need to just . . ."

And that's how a brilliant military operation ends. With one embarrassing phone call from your mother to the enemy.

Dr. Gristle's electronic service fields the call, which is played over my mother's feed.

"We are sorry. Due to a serious set of circumstances, Dr. Gristle is not currently available to handle your call. In case of an emergency, please leave your —"

My mother terminates the communication. Yesss. Oh. But then again, the situation he is addressing is my friends.

"Oh, is that right?" My mother, onscreen, is staring at the general vicinity of the doctor's impersonal message. "Too busy to take my call, Doctor-I-Wanna-Be-a-Star? We'll see about this."

Yes, my Newsmama is now fully engaged in the righteous battle. The fact that she is enraged over getting her call screened is not important.

"Hi, hon," That Voice says through the ceiling speaker.

"Hi, pet," she says. "Listen, we have to take care of this situation right now. It is making poor Zany sick. Somebody has to go down with him right now to Dr. Gristle's office and get them to let us look at their tracking equipment."

"Oh," Dad says. "Now as in . . . now. Right. Tight morning, hon. Tight, tight . . ."

"Call it up," she says.

Instantly, two of the screens on opposite walls switch to reveal parallel sections of their calendars. Their schedules meet across an uncrowded room.

"Twelve thirty is no good here."

"One fifteen . . . if this guy doesn't show up again . . . can't count on that, though."

I fall back on my bed and start cleaning my face like a

cat, licking my paws and rubbing, to see if anyone notices. Right.

"Let's take this to the greenroom," my mother says, and both of them pop off.

The greenroom is their language for taking the convo off-line, away from me, into a different channel.

In a second, they're back.

"Right," Newsmama says. "This is really bad. Couldn't have picked a worse day."

"Too true," That Voice says. "Do you think, honestly, he would notice if we just got a new Hugo? Do you remember what color he was?"

I really almost hate to end it.

"Um, guys," I say, "you kind of missed the greenroom. You're back in my room."

That Voice says, "Goodness."

My Newsmama gets absolutely flustered. She blinks twice and has to move a swatch of hair off her temple. But she bounces all the way back.

"Okay, sweetie. Right. Have your people meet my people —"

"Mom?" I say, waving at her and smiling.

"Of course. Sorry, honey. Have your*self* meet *my*self at Dr. Gristle's office in twenty minutes."

There, now. The word is love.

When we meet outside the Dr. G. Center, the place is locked up, and there is a note on the glass saying basically the same thing as the recorded message. My mother responds by repeating, basically, her message.

"Open up, Gary." She is pounding on the door. "We need you right now, so don't try the veterinary diva routine today unless you want to do your next broadcast in front of twelve people on the community pet search program."

I'm sure they are monitoring activity here at the front entrance, based on the speed with which the front door flies open.

Behind me, a chubby rat in a vest, who has spoken to a certain dog, lets himself in with very little fanfare.

"Hellooo," Dr. Gristle says, gracious yet sweat-covered and shifty. He shoots me a glance then gets right back to Newsmama. "Whatever can I do for you?"

Behind him, the place is a beehive of activity. Oddly for a vet center there is not an animal in sight. Despite the place being closed to the public, there are more humans in here than on any day I've been here before. Uniform types are flitting about, conferring, ducking into rooms. Very serious hushy-discushy behavior fills the place. I can see that my mother's newshound instincts are perked — for a second.

"My boy has lost his dog, Doctor, and I believe one of your fabulous contraptions can bring him back."

"Oh," he says, "absolutely. But you know those silly

mutts. They do this all the time. They scamper off and then wander back and . . . we're in a kind of a state here today."

"You know," Neswmama says, all steel and mean politeness, "one of those doohickeys you were crowing about on my program? I was certain that was the answer."

She is looking over his shoulder again, at the curious buzz of very serious activity. The enemy is planning its attack, and we are standing in their central command.

"Oh, of course," the good doctor says, then practically drags me down the hall to the place we want to go. I notice my mother noticing as she lags behind, eyeing the place up and down and sideways. Discreetly, she talks into this little device in her watch. It takes memos. Then it sends the memos to her office.

"Find your mutt and get out," he hisses in my ear. "No joke, Zane, this is far bigger than both of us, and right now you and I are both in serious jeopardy."

Now, I am scared.

"Where's the gizmo, Gary?" Mom says. "We don't have to make a big production out of this."

"It's here," he says, standing defensively in front of a big metal door.

"So?" she says, checking her watch. "Let's go."

"Oh, you can't possibly —"

It's time for me to lay it on thick. "Mom! I'm starting to really worry about Hugo. If anything has happened to him . . ."

"Gary," she says to Gristle curtly, gesturing at the door, "you like the bright lights?"

The door opens.

We are standing in front of a wall of data, fronted by a chair and a keyboard. Gristle throws himself into the chair, click-clicks, and a massive map of the area comes up.

"Tell us how it works," Mom says.

"I cannot tell you."

She takes out her professional electronic notepad to show she means business.

"Tell us how it works," she says again, this time in media-shmooze.

"Well," he says, "you plug this field of data into this field of geographical mapping, cross it with this database of logged individual client creatures . . ."

Five ego-drenched minutes later, I have the raw info I need. I absorb it with ease, thanks to all those hours of my life spent *not* playing baseball or guitar or surfing anything that required an actual surfboard. Enter my friend, Rattus. He looks up at me from the base of the doorway, smiling. "Ya know, Zane," he says, "sometimes I think I should be hurt, the way I can cruise through a busy place like this with nobody even noticing I exist. But then again . . . shall we commence this operation?"

"Commence."

Rattus is a one-rat Special Ops. In less than a minute, he gets into the animal cage area and deftly unlatches each and every gate. The animals are out, and they are excited.

Mayhem erupts in the hallways of the world center of animal control technology, as the whole place spins right *out* of control. Gristle, Mom, and I dash into the corridor to see what's going on, and right away I realize the situation is more thrillingly chaotic than even I dared hope.

Doctor G-for-Greedy just cannot leave well enough alone. He has replaced the first batch of escapee animals with a more diverse bunch who may look thrilling to his masters when they are in their cages, but look like not a lot of fun running in the hallways. There is a badger, chasing a giant nurse up onto a desk. There is a three-foot gator dripping attitude along the baseboards. There are a pair of spider monkeys with teeth that never seem to show up on posters, but are front and center now. I don't know what the conditions were in that room, but there are enough angry, clued-in animals shaking this place down to form a very impressive state militia. And in the spirit of the occasion, both domestic and exotic are working in such harmony to terrorize the humans. Really, it's heartwarming.

"My lord, what is going on in this place?" Newsmama demands.

This scares Gristle more than the lynx who is padding toward us with a Dr. G. related traumatic-stress episode written across his smiley face.

"Nothing at all. These animals are all here for legitimate research reasons. We'll round them up as soon —"

The lynx seems to have had a sudden clear flashback and needs to see the doctor immediately, without an appointment. Gristle runs in the opposite direction. Lynx, dashing past, gives me a wink and an "oh, mee-yow."

My mother takes the opportunity to flee the other way, toward the door. "Come on, Zane," she says.

I stand and watch until she is out the door. It'll be a while before she notices I'm not there.

In a flash, I am back in the computer room, the door shut behind me, and I'm working the controls. I call up the individual listing of tagged animals, presented by species and serial number. Domestics also have personal details. But the list is so long, way beyond what I expected. He must have thousands of these things going. I would never be able to sort through and figure out who is who.

I switch over to geographical view.

There we are. The map centers on the center here. I scan out, scan over. Better, better . . .

"Oh, dear, mercy, no . . ." I hear as somebody bounces off the door behind me and receives a talking to from a big angry dog.

I hover over the general area, I zoom in. There it is. There.

The WildWood. Even from the air, even on a map on a screen inside the worst building in the world, the WildWood is a haunting, gorgeous place. The WildWater sits there, glistening in the center of it, and I can all but taste it from where I sit.

I lean forward, almost to touching the place, and I breathe it in.

I can smell it. I can smell the green and the wet and the thick clay dirt of the place and I just want to freeze it all and everything right here right now.

But I can't freeze everything, can I?

I back away from the screen and focus back on the job at hand. Looking over the WildWood scene again, the point of it all makes itself very clear.

One by one by one, they come sparking to life. Twinkling like tiny stars in the universe of the WildWood, all my chipped forest friends come clear and bright and sparkling on the screen. There they are, slowly moving west, to the edge of the woods, toward the WildArea beyond.

I highlight the map, and call up the details. A blizzard

of facts float across my vision as all the animals in that area become known to me. Bingo.

In no order, I gather them all up, corral them into a file, and give the command.

DISCONNECT FROM GRID.

The system would like a word with me.

DISCONNECT ALL FROM GRID?

YES.

ARE YOU SURE YOU WANT TO DISCONNECT ALL FROM GRID?

The madness outside has reached such shrieky proportions that it cannot go on much longer. It sounds like pro wrestling and the African wildlife exhibit at the zoo were thrown together in a big jar and shaken up vigorously.

Shut up already and **YES, DISCONNECT ALL FROM GRID.** Why can't machines just shut up and do what they are told?

Finally, in a flash, the tiny twinkling lights push way up bright, then go down, and out.

I feel a big smile unfurl across my face. "Off you go, friends."

For the first time in my life, I feel like I have *done* something. I'm almost going to pass out with the rush and the thrill of it.

I burst out of that room to find mostly animals left patrolling the corridors. No doubt reinforcements are on the way for all the big babies cowering in the various offices so the time to scram is now.

Rattus finds me and looks about as happy as I am.

"Good job," I say. "Now, one more thing —"

"I have some wires to chew?"

"Yup. You have some wires to chew."

He heads into the control room.

At the end of the corridor, I see my mother. She is outside with her back to the glass. She is doing a live report.

That's my Newsmama.

Somebody must have signaled her because she turns her back to the camera (*back* to the camera? My mom?), and checks me coming her way.

The look of astonishment on her face catches me by surprise. Then I get it.

The corridor, jam-packed with creatures great and small, has gone totally docile. They all just hang there, cool as cats, and let me make my way right down the middle of them.

"Thanks, guys," I say. "You are heroes, every one. We will be back for you when it's not so dangerous, I promise."

None of them actually speak to me, but they let out a simultaneous roar-screech, a kind of victory cheer in their animal tongues.

I push my way out the door and find my hard-to-impress mother slack-jawed.

"They didn't bother you at all," she says.

"Of course not," I say. "You know I'm good with animals."

She stares at me blankly. I point back at the camera. "You'd better get to work," I say as a cheeky monkey throws himself at the glass door and does something quite rude in his bid for stardom.

Newsmama faces the camera, and I slip away.

BLUETOOTH IS FREE

There is no time. This much I know. As I enter the WildWood, all I want to do is establish for myself that the animals have gotten free and safe and no matter what when Gristle and his Gristlies show up, they will not be taking any of my friends back with them.

I have faith in Hugo, I do. I want to see this for myself.

I wonder if he stuck around. He was here, after all, when I freed all the animals in the WildWood. If he wanted to be found at this point, it would be his decision.

If I were him, I would go. I would live in the WildArea.

"Zane! Is that you, Zane?"

I believe that is a Yorkshire accent in my ear noodle.

I go running at the sound of his voice — just the way a dog is supposed to come running to the sound of his "master's" voice — and scratch myself to pieces getting to him. I am thrilled when I emerge into a small clearing and find him.

But then it goes different.

Hugo is not alone. He is just about alone, but not quite.

Hugo is half-lying across the flattened body of Bluetooth. I drop down to them, pat Hugo's big beautiful face, then lay a hand across Bluetooth's very visible ribs.

There is some warmth. There is some beat. Just.

He is lying on his side as flat as he could be on a bedding of pine needles. His eyes are closed tight, his tongue is hanging so completely out of the side of his mouth it's like it is trying desperately to escape a sinking ship. The tip of his tongue touches the ground. . . .

From above, with the Earth as a backdrop, he looks like he could be mid-run, his fine fit legs spaced in perfect stride. From ground level, though, which is where I am when I crouch beside him, he is a most unnatural sight. His head, his shoulders, his ribs hug flat to the ground as if he's been steamrolled, but those thighs on those back legs rise from the earth like mini mountains.

His teeth are bared, just the way they are when they are muzzled and striving in the heat of a race. Desperate.

I pick up the old champion and rest him across my lap as I sit on the ground. I know there is nothing I can do for him except make sure he doesn't die alone.

I only hope he can know that. I only hope that while I am holding him, and while Hugo is leaning into him, he can know that we are here to see him out and see that he doesn't have to be scared.

And I want to apologize to him for what people have done to him, for the race that started that would only stop this way.

"I'm sorry," I say.

Hugo nestles in closer to Bluetooth.

"He only ever wanted to be a dog," Hugo says. "He never wanted to be a machine."

"Did everybody else get away okay?" I ask.

"Clean break," Hugo says. "At least, there's that."

"There is that."

I am sure I know the moment when he is gone. A little shallow breath, a tiny shallow breath, expands his ribs. And then, nothing. He is done. Free.

Eventually, I get up and select a spot. Underneath a twisty hazel tree that looks like a nice forever resting spot for a dog who had more than his share of unrest. I get on all fours and I start digging, using a sharp rock, my fingers . . . and my friend.

At first, I am digging silly, dog-style but not that well. Then Hugo is beside me, and we do about as well as two sad gravedigger dogs can do.

It's raggedy, but good. I carry Bluetooth to it, feeling his strong, hard, empty self. I want to pump him back up, squeeze him and shake him, talk to him, breathe warm breath on his face and somehow coax him back with my assurance that everything will be better this time around because we know better now, and I am here now and promising to keep an eye on things.

But I can't do that, and I know it. I lay him gently in the hole and stand in there with him for a few seconds, feeling like somehow I should be doing something more here, like I owe him something more but I have no idea what.

I pat him. Two, three, four, five strokes of his coat, from the side of his sleek bullet head over all the bumpy bones and muscles back to those amazing thighs.

"See ya, boy," I say as I stroke him a last time and sit back on the edge of his open grave.

I didn't even know him, really.

And yet. Here I am, saying good-bye, and suddenly crying so sloppily I'm ashamed to let my own dog see me.

Hugo comes close and does what dogs do so well. He sits just next to me, his side bumped against my side. His warm little self comforting my foolish sad self.

I lay our friend in the grave, and climb out, only to find an even worse nightmare waiting for me. Dr. Gristle is standing there under the twisted hazel tree. Standing behind him are a dozen or more apey-looking guys in weird military-medical space suits and goggles that reflect back at you.

"This was one creature who couldn't run and hide when I approached," he says. "Nice to see you again, Bluetooth." He hops into the hole and pulls out a scalpel.

"No!" I scream. "Leave him alone, you awful ghoul. Can't you for once leave him alone?" Two of the Gristlies are on me and have me in a clamp so tight there might actually be polar bears in those suits.

"This is no ordinary chip," he says, quickly scooping his prize, bagging it, and putting the bag in his pocket. "You saw how he ran. You saw where the science was going. You can't just bury that in the ground."

"Leave him alone," is all I can manage to say, but I say it with everything I have. I don't know what I have to back it up with, but my little dog is growling for ten. One big Gristlie grabs Hugo, squeezing him with one arm and muzzling him with the other hand.

Dr. Gristle climbs up out of the grave, leaving Bluetooth lying there — bony, cold, alone, naked.

"You'll see, Zane, eventually. You will see what it all means. You are just a kid now, but someday you will grow up and you will be able to understand how this is all so much bigger than we are. Then, you'll see it like I see it. And you will do things differently."

"I guess I'd better not grow up, then," I say.

"Oh, you'll grow up. But the way things look now, you might do your growing up in captivity. You have done some bad things, Zane, and I am afraid there is a price to pay."

He makes a truly hateful little dismissive wave motion, and the Gristlies haul me and Hugo away.

ISOLATION STATION

I am not under real arrest because I am too young for that. But it has been made abundantly clear to me how serious they consider the things I have done.

I am under house arrest. My room is still wired. Rewired — hyper-wired, in fact, to include dazzling new features.

Such as the Lock-and-Key Protocol™. That means my room is now an isolation chamber. I need electronic permission to get out. If I desire to leave, my request has to follow very rigid coding, must be submitted in advance, and must mesh with my schedule, which, of course, my room has in great detail. If all is not in order, if the correct procedure is not combined with a verifiable pretty-darned-compelling reason, it's lockdown. My door will not open. This is how it is going to be for two months. For starters. Even my schooling happens right here in my room, via technology.

I have made some people very angry.

I see nobody in the flesh. I am worried nauseous about what is becoming of the animals, but I am suffering a total blackout on communication with them.

And that includes my own dog.

I have not seen Hugo in a week, not since they dragged us away from Bluetooth's grave. My parents tell me he is receiving treatment for some unspecified malady and I will see him soon, but nothing gives me a good feeling these days.

If Gristle and company wanted to build for me a perfect personalized hell, they have succeeded.

And, of course, that is precisely what they wanted.

I am lying on my back, on my bed, which is mostly what I do now. My eyes are closed, which is mostly what they are now.

"Zany," comes That Voice out of the ceiling speaker. I have never felt less Zany in my unZany life. I don't even bother answering.

"I know you are angry, Son. But we cannot move forward if you are not going to take responsibility for your actions. I appreciate that you do not understand Dr. Gristle's work. But the important thing is, you don't have to understand it. You have no idea how much trouble those missing animals have caused."

Missing! So they're still missing!

"There are a great many people who believe that work is of supreme importance, and the fact that you disagree does not give you license to go undermining adults and the government and such. That is simply not the way civilized society works."

"Could you define *civilized* for me, Dad?" I challenge.

There is a big fat silence in the room that suits me fine.

"Right," he says then, "I can see today won't be a leaps-and-bounds progress day, so I'll just let it go for the time being. I just wanted to tell you to go to your door. It'll be unlocked for thirty seconds. You have a visitor."

I bolt, of course, because any visitor not named Gristle is a welcome visitor. I race to the door.

And stop short. It could well be him. They would do this *for my own good*.

I'm frozen.

The seconds tick away: 22, 23, 24 . . .

Once it's locked again, it will stay that way, no matter who's out there.

I throw it open on twenty-eight.

"Hugooo!" I holler, scooping him up in my arms and rushing him into my room before anything bad can happen. The door slams shut and locks.

I squeeze him and I squeeze him and I squeeze him, making it impossible for him to talk if he wanted to. "I missed you so much," I say, holding him up in front of me so his nose is touching mine. "I have been so lonely, I can't tell you."

He gives my nose a little lick. I laugh, put him on the

floor. I run and get my ear noodle, jam it in, and stand before him. "Tell me everything," I say. "Tell me the whole week. Where were you, what did they do? They didn't hurt you, did they?"

I wait anxiously.

And I wait more anxiously.

He gives me his glorious, magnificent quizzical head-tilt with his glorious, magnificent head.

And that's all he gives me.

"Hugo?" I say, though I already know. "Hugo? Tell me something, pal. Tell me any something you can."

He just stares at me.

I just stare at him.

Together.

In solitary confinement.

I reach down and get two good fistfuls of beautiful white wiry face-hair.

"This is not the last word," I promise him.

He licks my nose to seal the deal.

End of Book One